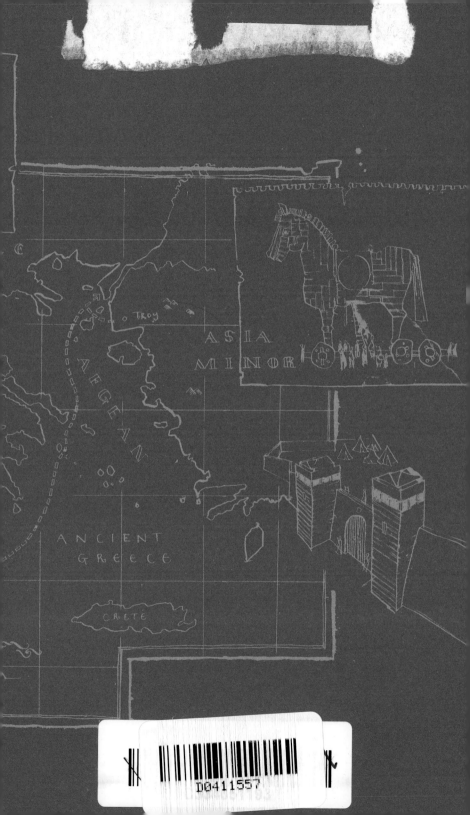

TROY

ASIA
MINOR

AEGEAN

ANCIENT
GREECE

CRETE

When Fishes Flew

Books by Michael Morpurgo

For Ali, Chris, Pip and Kate.
Thank you.
—Michael Morpurgo

First published in Great Britain by
HarperCollins *Children's Books* in 2021
HarperCollins *Children's Books* is a division of HarperCollins*Publishers* Ltd
1 London Bridge Street
London SE1 9GF

www.harpercollins.co.uk

HarperCollins*Publishers*
1st Floor, Watermarque Building, Ringsend Road
Dublin 4, Ireland

1

HB ISBN 978-0-00-835218-9
TPB ISBN 978-0-00-845465-4
PB ISBN 978-0-00-852034-2

Michael Morpurgo and George Butler assert the moral right to be identified
as the author and illustrator of the work respectively.

A CIP catalogue record for this title is available from the British Library.

Typeset in Horley Old Style 11pt/22pt

Printed and bound in the UK using 100% renewable electricity
at CPI Group (UK) Ltd

Conditions of Sale

michael morpurgo

When Fishes Flew

THE STORY OF ELENA'S WAR

Illustrated by George Butler

HarperCollins *Children's Books*

My Glowing Globe

I blame the globe, my glowing globe – and the flying fish.

But I suppose I should also blame Elena, my great-aunt, who gave me the globe in the first place. She started this story and she ended it too. When I say blame, I don't mean blame, not really. I mean that without the globe and without my great-aunt, none of the rest of this story would ever have happened. And it did happen.

The flying fish happened, really happened. I'm telling you, I saw him. Often. I was there. But more of him later. A lot more.

It was also my great-aunt who first gave me my name. My real name is Amanda. But, whenever she came to stay with us when I was little, she always called me Nandi. I liked that a lot better than Amanda, or Mandy – which most people seemed to want to call me. So I told everyone at school and at home that I was Nandi, and that I wouldn't answer to any other name. I've been Nandi ever since.

My great-aunt Elena – Auntie Ellie, I called her – came to stay with us about once every two years or so in our house in St Kilda in Melbourne, Australia. I longed for her visits because she always brought me interesting things from where she lived, which was far, far away, on a Greek island called Ithaca. Every time she came, there would be presents: always Greek honey from her own bees for Papa, herbs from her garden for Ma – oregano and *sapsychos*. (Meatballs mixed with *sapsychos* cooked on the barbecue was my all-time favourite – still is.)

But the best gift she ever gave me was my glowing globe. There was a light inside, so my globe was a night-light too. Auntie Ellie laughed a lot, talked quietly to me, listened to me and, when we went on walks along the Yarra River, she would often swing my hand, and I loved that.

I treasured everything she gave me as I was growing up: my T-shirt with a Greek ship sailing across a deep blue sea, and another one with the huge wooden

horse of Troy being hauled in through the gates of the city by those poor deluded Trojans. Then there was the silver dolphin and the small bronze statue of a helmeted Greek warrior from ancient times, his sword raised to fight off some hideous monster. She told me his name was Odysseus, and that he was born in Ithaca, like she was. These were my favourite things in all the world.

It was my Auntie Ellie who first introduced me to the story of Odysseus – for her, and soon for me, the

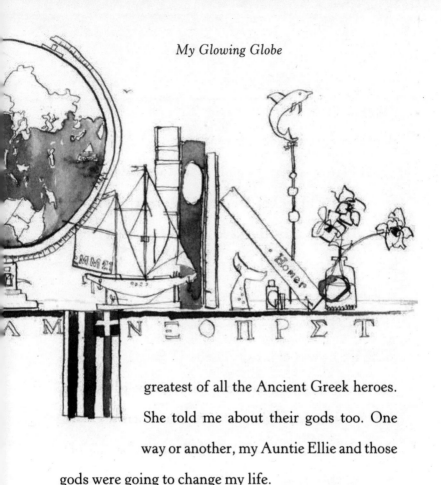

greatest of all the Ancient Greek heroes. She told me about their gods too. One way or another, my Auntie Ellie and those gods were going to change my life.

My silver dolphin and my precious statue of Odysseus lived on the chest of drawers in my bedroom on either side of my glowing globe. I saw them when I woke in the morning, and they were the last things I saw at night. I don't remember when exactly, on which visit, she gave me the globe. I must have been too

11

young to remember, or maybe it's because her visits, all of them memorable, blur into one.

All I know is that the globe was always there, that I grew up with it, looked at it every day, touched it, spun it, went to sleep and dreamed my dreams in its glow. I travelled in my mind to every continent on that globe, sailed all the seven blue seas.

Before I left to go to school every morning, I would touch the helmet of my Odysseus – fifteen centimetres tall, no more – and give the globe a gentle spin for luck. I loved making the world turn before my eyes. I imagined how the Greek gods must have loved that too. My globe was in the room with me while I did my homework, as I listened to my music, when I did my reading and my dreaming. And, because my globe glowed in the dark, it was a comfort to me at night-times too. For me, my world was never just St Kilda or Melbourne or Australia. They were my home. But my world was my globe and, from a very young age, all I wanted to do was to grow up fast, go travelling and explore it.

Whenever she came to stay, Auntie Ellie would read to me every night before I went to sleep. She read in such a wonderfully confidential tone, with a deep, sonorous voice that suited perfectly the epic and often tragic stories of her heroes, and mine too. She would read with intensity and passion, living every word, so that I did too – and always in her heavy Greek accent, of course.

It was mostly through Auntie Ellie's visits that I came to know anything of the family story, how and why we were living in Australia. Papa had emigrated from Greece. Auntie Ellie had told me it was because of an earthquake. The family house on Ithaca had been destroyed, so they had to leave when Papa was a very small boy. He had hardly any memories of it, he told me. He had come only with his father, and he didn't like to talk about him, or about his mother, my grandmother. All I knew about them was that my grandfather was called Manos, my grandmother Zita, and that she had died a long, long time ago, before Papa ever came over to Australia.

Auntie Ellie told me a little more about Manos, her younger brother, that they grew up together, did everything together. But Manos too had died before I was born. I knew him and my grandmother only from photos, which Auntie Ellie showed me. But she, like Papa, did not seem to like to speak of them. So I knew nothing more about either of my grandparents. It was almost as if they'd never been. People you see only in photos and you've never known are never real to you. I loved their names, Manos and Zita, and always wish I'd known them.

Both Auntie Ellie and Papa were more than happy to remind me where I came from. Papa in particular was very proud of being Greek. He had a very Greek name: Jason. The first story of the Greek heroes Auntie Ellie ever told me was Jason and the Argonauts, and his search for the Golden Fleece. But to me he was never Jason, just

Papa, a Greekish papa, but also Australian. He spoke English much like everyone else I knew, much like Ma – who had come from Ireland, by the way, when she was little. Auntie Ellie was really Greek, properly Greek.

Ma had a fine Irish name. She was called Grania, who was an Irish heroine, just as important and heroic as Jason, she would insist, whenever she thought Papa and I were both becoming a bit too Greek. Papa always insisted he was a Greek under his skin, in his heart. 'Australian outside, Greek inside,' was what he used to tell me. And I think that's what I was already becoming too, but I didn't tell Ma.

Even after I was way past the age to be read to, when I was reading books by myself, I loved to listen to Auntie Ellie reading to me. I loved all her Greek stories, especially the tale of Odysseus, of the Trojan Wars and his ten-year journey home to Ithaca, after the siege of Troy. By the time I was ten or eleven, I knew the names of all the Greek islands he visited on his way back home, all his adventures, and all the Greek gods who made life so hard for him. And these fickle, interfering gods? Believe me, they really knew how to make things difficult.

Proteus, son of Poseidon, was my favourite Greek god because he could change who he was: he could metamorphose, become whoever and whatever he wanted to be. I was fascinated by that, as I was by all the one-eyed or many-headed monsters that brave Odysseus had to confront on his journey home. In time, Auntie Ellie had told me all about the gods and their mischievous machinations, all the devious games they played with the lives of Greeks and Trojans. I discovered how kings and queens and princes and princesses, all my great heroes and heroines, seemed to be little more than puppets manipulated by these scheming gods. They were not likeable in the least, except Proteus.

But the more I heard Auntie Ellie's stories of all these Ancient Greek gods and heroes, especially Proteus and Odysseus, the more I was coming to love the idea of being Greek. Every time Auntie Ellie came to stay, she would teach me a few more words of Greek, and bring more books for me to read, mostly books about Odysseus, about Ithaca. She taught me the letters of the Greek alphabet, to write them and pronounce them. She taught me to speak my first Greek words: *kalimera*, good morning. *Efharisto*, thank you. *Ellas*, Greece. *Adio*, goodbye. *Kalinikta*, goodnight. I'd practise my words again and again at night in bed, looking at my glowing globe, longing to go there, to Greece, when I grew up.

Auntie Ellie would remind me often – she did repeat herself a bit, but I didn't mind: 'It's where your Greek family, your papa's family, comes from. And it's where Odysseus came from too. Never forget that, Nandi. One day you must come to Ithaca to visit. We have flying fish there, you know, and dolphins. Oh, and my bees. I sell their honey all over the island. Without my bees, I wouldn't be there. I save all my honey money to buy my plane ticket to come to Australia. You're my only family, you know. But it's always worth it, Nandi, just to see you.'

'We've got bees too, in Australia,' I told her. 'And flying fish and dolphins.'

'Of course you have, Nandi,' she said. 'I live on an island; you live on an island. Australia is a little bigger maybe than Ithaca. But you have sea all round just the same, don't you? And, where there's sea, there's dolphins and flying fish. And, where there's islands, there's bees, thank goodness – the world couldn't do without bees – but no honey is as good as mine. Keeps me young, keeps me strong.'

I knew about bees pollinating plants, of course,

and how important they were for growing things, but somehow I had never thought of Australia as an island till Auntie Ellie told me. Australia always seemed smaller to me after she said that. So much that she told me made me think again about the world, about myself.

Ithaca and Zorba

There is a whole community of Greek Australians living in Melbourne. And we are proud of it, our Greekness. We speak Australian, of course – well, English really. But only Auntie Ellie spoke English like a real Greek person. At home, even when she wasn't with us, we sometimes tried to be like her – properly

Greek. We supported Greece in the Olympics, or when they played football – even when they played against Australia or Ireland, which Ma didn't like much, but she wasn't that interested in football anyway.

We ate Greek salad often – too often – always with feta cheese and tomatoes and cucumber and onions. Calamari and moussaka. Meatballs with the *sapsychos* that Auntie Ellie brought us from her home in Ithaca, were firm favourites, and with chips, of course. We would often play Greek music and dance all together round the barbecue – Greek dancing, the *sirtaki*, Auntie Ellie called it, her favourite dance. We often danced when family and friends came round, at Christmas and on birthdays, but always when we were welcoming Auntie Ellie on the first evening she arrived.

We often played music by Mikis Theodorakis. She loved it when we all danced to his music, especially the *sirtaki* dance from the film *Zorba the Greek*. We would watch that at least once during her visit, and she always cried quietly. She wasn't sad, I felt, but moved, deeply moved, by the music, the landscape, by Greece. It all seemed to mean so much to her.

Her eyes were often bright with tears of joy, or of sadness – I was never sure which.

'Zorba's Dance' became my favourite piece of music to listen to when she wasn't there. Up in my room, I would close my eyes and dance, imagining I was on a beach in Greece, the beach I'd seen in *Zorba the Greek*, and I'd be dancing with Auntie Ellie, side by side, arms round one another's shoulders, dipping to the rhythm, clicking my fingers like she did. For me, it was always her tune, and I loved it because of that.

The truth was though that I only felt I was truly Greek when Auntie Ellie was there. I missed her so much when she wasn't with us. The spirit went out of the house somehow, the Greekness. We did Skype or Zoom with her sometimes, at Christmas, on birthdays, but she found it very difficult to make the technology work in Ithaca – and anyway it wasn't the same as having her there in the house. She never phoned, and we never phoned her. We all knew that she hated the phone. She told me once it was because she liked to see the faces of the people she was talking to, and it only made her sad to hear our voices and not be able to see us.

She would send us letters and postcards, lots of postcards, always of Ithaca. Ithaca was everywhere in our house in Melbourne, all over my bedroom walls, pinned up on the noticeboard in the kitchen, propped up on the mantelpiece in the sitting room. I would often take them down to read them,

and that wasn't always easy. As she got older, her handwriting became more and more wobbly. But whenever I read the postcards I could always hear her wonderful voice in her wobbly words. Sometimes I felt she was so close to me then, in the room with me almost.

Auntie Ellie was always old to me, maybe the oldest person I knew. But you should have seen her doing her Greek dancing! She danced so joyfully. She danced better than Papa or Ma, or any of their friends. Light on her feet, she seemed to float over the ground. And she swam in the sea every day, in her dress. She always wore black, a long black dress, and a black scarf that she would let me wear sometimes. I felt so Greek in her scarf.

She wore black because she was a widow – Ma told me that. Her husband, my great-uncle Alexis, had died when he was very young, she said, less than a year after they were married. I asked what had happened to him, but either Papa and Ma did not know, or they just wouldn't tell me. I never knew which. I didn't want to ask Auntie Ellie because I thought it would make her sad.

I longed to dance like her, to do it as easily and naturally as she did, and I longed to learn how to speak English like her so that I sounded Greek. I used to practise both my dancing and my speaking down at the bottom of our garden where no one could see or hear me. But, when I danced, I could never float over the ground like she did, and when I tried to speak like her, or try out the few Greek words she had taught me, I just sounded silly. So I very soon gave up.

And how I loved the honey she brought us, the honey her bees had made on Ithaca. We kept it as long as we could, eked it out. For me, a taste of that honey was a taste of Ithaca, of her world, another world I longed to go to. And I loved the idea that it was her honey that made the 'honey money', that she was saving up to fly over to see us the next time.

I still have most of my childhood treasures: the glowing globe, the silver dolphin and my Odysseus statue. They still live side by side in my room, but on a different chest of drawers, and in a different house, in a different country, on a different continent. Sometimes it feels like a different planet.

I'm looking at them right now as I am writing this. On my bed. I always write on my bed. It's more comfortable this way, propped on my pillows. I can concentrate better, dream better, remember better. And I can go off to sleep whenever I get tired. I'm getting tired now.

I keep wanting to tell you about the flying fish. But this is not the time. Not yet. Anyway, it would spoil the story if I told you now. So you're just going to have to wait.

The Letter from Auntie Ellie

I remember Ma telling me the news at breakfast one morning before I went off to school. I had just started at secondary school by then, so I must have been about twelve. It was the worst news. Auntie Ellie had written us a letter. Ma read it out to us. I don't remember the words. All I knew by the end of the letter was that

Auntie Ellie had decided that, as much as she wanted
to, she felt she couldn't come to stay with us any more,
that she was getting too old anyway to make the long
journey by air from Ithaca to Australia. But she also
said that she'd been worrying more and more that
flying round the world was not something she should
be doing any more. The threat of global warming,

the terrible bush fires we'd had in Australia, the flooding and the droughts that she'd seen on television – all of this had made up her mind not to fly again.

As Ma read the letter, Papa was sitting there at the table, looking as sad as I felt. I often forgot she was his aunt, but I was reminded now. I couldn't stop my eyes filling with tears. Ma could see I was upset too. She went on to explain to me how all good things have to come to an end, that we just had to accept that Auntie Ellie was an old lady now, that she was right about flying and global warming, that this moment was bound to come anyway one day, that travel was always going to be more and more difficult for her as she got older.

As the implications of this dreadful news sank in, it felt to me as if someone, something – fate, the gods – had taken scissors to my life and just cut it, cut me off from Auntie Ellie, from Greece, from Ithaca, from all the stories of Odysseus and Proteus, from my whole childhood.

'She can still Skype us, though, or Zoom us, can't she?' I said, fighting back the tears.

They kept looking at one another. 'Not really, Nandi,' replied Ma. 'You know she doesn't like all this technology. She says that whenever we do it she misses us more afterwards. And she doesn't like phoning either. You know that. She thinks it's expensive too, and it's not. But she won't listen. She has a mind of her own. She's like that.'

'But that doesn't mean we can't Skype her, does it?' I insisted. They didn't answer, but kept looking at one another. 'And we could go and see her instead. We could!'

After long moments, Ma told me: 'We couldn't afford it, Nandi. It would cost the earth for us all to fly there.'

I knew from their faces there was something else they didn't want to talk about. They were deciding which of them should tell me.

It was Papa who spoke up in the end.

'The thing is –' he began hesitantly. 'The thing is, Nandi, we didn't want to worry you, but last week Auntie Ellie had a fall. Quite a bad fall. She hit her head and now she doesn't see at all well, she says. Reading is hard for her. And she has dizzy spells. She even rang up, so we knew something had to be wrong. We didn't like to tell you till we'd found out more about how she was. You mustn't worry. She's made a great recovery, still a bit dizzy sometimes, but she's much better. Seeing a bit better again now too. She's walking fine, a bit shaky, but she's okay. I told her – we both told her – that she must come and live with us here. We're the only family she's got. But she won't hear of it. Ithaca is her home, she said, and she has good friends around her on the island, and that's where she belongs, where she's lived all her life. She wants to stay at home. She's also been saying for a while now, in her cards and letters, that there's something important she's got to do, and she has to stay in Greece to do it.'

'What?' I asked. 'Why? What's so important?'

'She won't say,' Ma went on. 'She's being very firm about it. She says she's not going to be a bother to anyone. And she doesn't want us feeling sorry for her or spending our "good, hard-earned money", as she calls it, flying out to Greece to see her. Her own words, Nandi. We can write to one another, she says. She's got that nice neighbour she's told us about, Maria, down the street, who looks after everything for her, and who speaks English, and can type for her whenever she wants to write us a letter if ever her writing gets a bit too wobbly. Anyway, one thing's for sure, and we have to get used to it: she won't be flying out here to visit us again. I'm sorry, Nandi. We're all sorry. But we've just got to accept it.'

I went off to school that day, heartbroken. The truth of it was hard to take in, hard to bear. I was never going to see Auntie Ellie again. Try as I might, I could not stop myself from breaking into sobs. The tears kept

coming. I decided I couldn't go into school that day.
I could not face my friends the way I was. Instead, I
would just walk around the city. So that's what I did,
for hours and hours, feeling about as miserable as I had
ever been.

A Flying Fish

Much of my walk took me alongside the Melbourne river, the Yarra. That got me thinking: this river flows into the sea, like all rivers. And, carried by the wind and the currents, this same water joins all the other great oceans of the world, which must in time flow into the sea around Ithaca. So the Yarra is like a pathway, a pathway to Ithaca and Auntie Ellie on the other side of the world. She looks out on the same sea, up at the same sky, the same moon and stars. Such thoughts as I walked along the river brought Auntie Ellie closer to me. I felt calmer and the tears stopped coming.

Then I saw the fish, the flying fish. I'd seen them before, by the sea, but not in the river. This one leaped up out of the water right in front of me, and flew off low over the river, on his way to the sea, on the way – I felt it at that moment, and was quite sure of it – to Auntie Ellie and Ithaca.

That was when my phone began buzzing in my pocket, went on and on buzzing at me. I didn't answer. I didn't even look at who was calling. I didn't want to know, didn't want to talk to anyone. I switched it off.

It was during that long day of wandering that I made up my mind what I would do. The flying fish had decided me. I would spread my wings and fly, just like him. Someday, some way, I would go to Ithaca and see Auntie Ellie.

When I left school in a few years' time, I would spin my globe for the last time, say goodbye to Ma and Papa, walk off down our road, and find my way over the sea to Ithaca, to Auntie Ellie. I would visit her, see her island home on the far side of the world, and discover where Odysseus had lived. I would walk where Odysseus had walked. It would be the adventure of my life. Yes, I would fly. Global warming was important, but seeing Auntie Ellie was much more important. That's how I felt, and I wasn't going to change my mind.

Meanwhile, I determined I would write to her often. I would send her lots of postcards of Australia, of the cities, the outback, the wild life, the kangaroos, the galahs, the kookaburras, the wombats. If she was having problems with her eyes still, that English-speaking neighbour of hers, Maria, could read them to her, and describe the pictures on the postcards. Auntie Ellie could pin them up in her house. So then we would have her Ithaca all over our house, and she would have our Australia all over hers.

I didn't know it at the time, of course, but I discovered later that while I was wandering along, lost in thoughts of Auntie Ellie and Ithaca, the secretary from school had already phoned Ma in the hospital where she worked to ask where I was, if anything was wrong, why I hadn't come to school that day. She told Ma that a teacher on her way to school had spotted me walking down by the river, and that I looked as if I'd been crying.

So, by the time I got home that afternoon, they were both frantic with worry. Papa was furious, but Ma just clung to me as if I'd been gone for a month. Papa went wild. He kept waving his arms and shouting at me, and made me promise never to do such a thing again. I promised. He ended up in tears then, we all did, and all our hugging told me I was forgiven. They knew why I was upset, why I'd run off. They understood.

The next morning, our head teacher, Mr Perkin – Peeky we called him – was not so understanding. I had a ticking-off from him in his office, but that was to be expected. It was his job after all. Peeky wasn't really cross, just pretending. I think Ma or Papa must have explained the reason I'd gone missing. I didn't know it then, of course, but that day I spent wandering along the Yarra River, that sighting of the flying fish, that day I decided to skip school, was to change my life for ever.

Stories and Heroes

It's strange how slowly the school years pass by when you're living them every day, but how fast they seem to have gone once they're over. I was suddenly seventeen, and walking out of the school gates for the last time, exams done, school done. All this while, I had been immersing myself more and more in the stories of Ancient Greece.

I had even studied some Ancient Greek at home, the language of my heroes and their gods, read the plays of great Greek writers, of Aeschylus and Sophocles, read Homer's *Odyssey* again and again, the best book I ever read. (I also discovered that Homer had lived on Ithaca, like Auntie Ellie, which was amazing! Maybe she had told me and I'd forgotten.)

I had tried to learn all I could about the history of Greece, ancient and modern, over thousands of years right up to the present day. It made me very proud and very connected to know that my home country, Australia, was a democratic country, like so many countries in the world, and that in countries like ours it was the people who decided how society and the laws should be, who should govern, and that this was only because the Ancient Greeks had pioneered the idea of democracy in Athens several thousand years before.

I had by now created a map that covered half my

bedroom wall, a map of the ten-year journey back home Odysseus had made, from island to island, after the Greeks' conquest of Troy. The story of that cunning and terrible victory – maybe the greatest hoax in all of history – had haunted me for years: how the Greeks left behind on the plain, which lay between the city walls of Troy and the sea beyond, a huge wooden horse, a parting gift to the people of Troy, a horse that was packed full of Greek soldiers armed to the teeth and ready to steal out at night and do their worst. I still had the T-shirt of that horse in my drawer, a bit small for me these days, but it was always for ever treasured.

I had seen it all often, in my mind, the whole story: of the Greeks sailing away in their ships, seemingly abandoning their tents, seemingly giving up the ten-year-long siege and going home, defeated. I had pictured the Trojans up on the walls of the city, rejoicing to see their enemy sail away after all the years of war

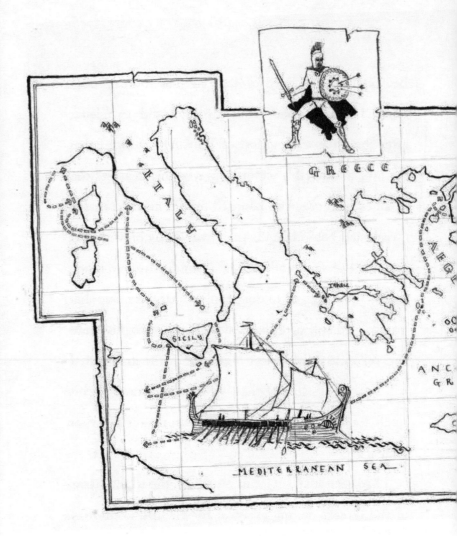

and siege, amazed and puzzled at this strange gift of
a giant wooden horse. And it was not hard either to
imagine the joy, and the relief, and the triumph, as they
hauled the giant Trojan horse in through their gates.

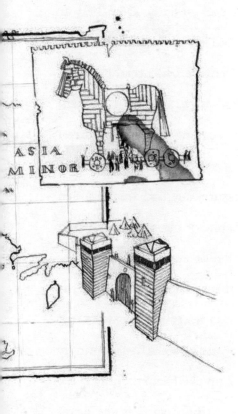

I had imagined it all, again and again, in my dreams, in my nightmares, how they must have celebrated that night, revelling in their victory, and how in the silence of the night they had climbed down out of the great horse, the Trojans still deep in drunken sleep, how they had opened the gates to let their army in, and the terrible slaughter and horror and burning that followed, as the vengeful Greeks sacked the city.

I knew from my map on the wall all the places at which Odysseus must have, or might have, stopped off on his way home after the sack of Troy, after the war was over, all the countries and islands he had visited – I had researched each one. Because I had read Homer's *Odyssey* again and again, in Ancient Greek, in English, I knew all the stories of his adventures on his long journey back to Ithaca to his long-suffering wife, Penelope; how, under relentless pressure, she had finally given in and promised to choose one of her many persistent and threatening suitors, but only, she told them, when she finished the tapestry she was weaving, and how she had cunningly unpicked her stitching every night so that she never finished it, and that way had kept her suitors at bay. In fact, the more I learned about Penelope, the more she became my hero too.

I even taught myself to weave, as Penelope had done – well, it was knitting really. I knitted a scarf, but like Penelope I always unpicked it just before I finished it. Then I'd start again, making it better each time. It was blue for Greece, and yellow for Australia. As the years passed, as I knitted and unpicked, knitted and unpicked, I came to admire Penelope much more than Odysseus. I loved him as you worship a hero, but – brave as he was – he was not always easy to like or admire. He was, I thought, rather too pleased with himself, dishonest and unfaithful, and could be horribly cruel.

He had a nasty streak, and heroes should not have nasty streaks.

Despite all that, he remained my greater hero. I was loyal to him, still am. But Penelope I admired. I admired her patience and loyalty as she waited for him to come home, her strength of mind to resist all her suitors, and she was cunning too, clever.

Every day, all through my schooldays, I looked at my glowing globe, that map on the wall, and at Auntie Ellie's postcards of Ithaca. That was where I was going, to see Auntie Ellie, to walk where Odysseus had walked, to where Penelope had waited for him. And I would take my lovely blue-and-yellow scarf with me, finished, and give it to Auntie Ellie. She had often said in her postcards how cold and damp winters were in Ithaca.

It was during these years that I realised more and more that I knew so little about Auntie Ellie. All I knew was that she was Greek, lived on an island called Ithaca, and was old, small, dark-skinned and wrinkled, a kindly great-aunt, who danced beautifully, elegantly, and that our home had always been a happier place with her there. She brought us life and laughter. But she had never once talked about herself or her own life. I often asked Ma and Papa about her. But they also seemed to know very little. She lived alone on Ithaca, a widow who had never married again after her young husband Alexis had died. She had no children, and was the only relative Ma and Papa had left living in Greece. That was about all they seemed to know about her, or all they would tell me.

To us, she was just our Auntie Ellie, who was far away and couldn't come to see us any more. We missed her, but we didn't know her. It was strange. In a way, she was the best and most constant friend I had ever had as I was growing up, but I knew hardly anything about her. She was a mystery.

But this was about to change. I was about to find out all about her, and in a way I could never have possibly imagined.

The Longest Journey

I remember Auntie Ellie once telling me, when I was quite little, that she thought of life as a long journey, but as an adventure too, and that we all have to be ready for it. I know now what she meant, but I don't think I did at the time. By the time I set off on my journey to Ithaca, on what turned out to be the great adventure of my life, I was still not at all ready. I thought I was, but I was wrong. But to be fair to me, nothing could ever have prepared me either for my life or my journey or my adventure, and certainly not for the flying fish.

The plan for the beginning of my journey I had thought through and worked out in detail. As soon as I had passed my exams and was able to leave school, I would have to go and earn some money. Air travel from Australia to Greece, from Melbourne to Athens, would be expensive – even the cheapest flights, I discovered. (I put global warming to the back of my mind. I know I shouldn't have, but I did.) From Athens, I could go by bus and boat to Ithaca. I wouldn't tell Auntie Ellie I was coming – I'd just turn up on her doorstep and surprise her. Ithaca was a small enough place. Only two or three thousand people lived there. Someone would know her. And I knew her address anyway, and the name of her friend, Maria, who lives just down the road from her. I could find her.

Once in Greece, I knew travelling around by bus would be cheap enough, but then I had to live, eat and sleep. It was all going to cost money. So that had to come first: I had to earn it somehow.

I didn't want to ask for any help from Papa and Ma because I knew they struggled anyway to make ends meet, and besides I did not want to involve them in my adventure. I didn't want to have to tell them exactly where I was going. If I told them I was planning to visit Auntie Ellie, they'd have let her know for sure. So I just said that I was going travelling, in Europe, like a lot of young Australians do – it's a sort of rite of passage for us – with only a large rucksack for company. It was all they needed to know, and all I was going to tell them. At last I would be out in the world on my own, and travelling around that glowing globe.

So I spent nine months working my socks off in a café down on the riverfront, which was hard on the feet, and meant lots of late nights. There were good days and bad – the tipping could be great sometimes – but there were also some really awkward customers too. You meet all sorts working in a café: lovely people, boring people, the good, the bad, the ugly, the beautiful. My workmates were fun, and the money in my bank account grew steadily. I was living at home, paying my way, walking to work. Hardly any living expenses to speak of. Nine months later, I had enough. Not plenty, but enough. I could go.

I had a feeling, spinning my globe as I left my room that last morning at home, that this was going to be a momentous journey, the adventure of a lifetime. I think that was why I had already decided I would write a diary, that taking pictures on my phone was not enough. I wouldn't write my diary necessarily every day, but whenever the mood took me, whenever there had been momentous happenings, so that I had a record of my journey to Ithaca and of everything that was going to happen to me there. It would be my very own odyssey. Not Homer's *Odyssey* but my odyssey to find the home of Odysseus and Penelope, and Homer himself, and my Auntie Ellie. Nandi's *Odyssey*.

So here it is, not all of it, not much of it, but just the few most extraordinary days of my odyssey, word for word, the whole incredible story just as I wrote it down. Some entries you will find quite short, some – when I couldn't stop writing because there was so much to tell – very long. That's just how it is with keeping a diary. You can follow where I went, if you like, on any map, Google or otherwise, on any globe, glowing or otherwise.

And no, I haven't forgotten the flying fish. You've had a glimpse of him already, but there's more of him to come, lots more. Promise.

My Odyssey

1 May 2011

I'm on the plane from Melbourne to Athens. Global warming is still on my mind – I can't keep it out. Don't feel good about it, but too late to turn back now. Ma cried saying goodbye at the airport. Which made me cry too. I promised myself I wouldn't, but I did. Her fault though. As Papa was hugging me, he whispered something in my ear. 'You give Auntie Ellie our love when you see her. Don't forget now.'

I didn't know what to say for a moment or two. I just said, 'Love you, Papa.'

'Me too,' he said.

When I walked away, I didn't turn and wave. I was crying buckets. Didn't want them to see.

I'm looking at the last postcard Auntie Ellie sent

me a few weeks ago. All she said was that her bees were doing well, making lots of honey, that she hoped I was happy working in the café and that she'd done that once when she was young like me. I could hear her voice in every wobbly word she wrote. It was a postcard I'd had before, of the harbour at Vathy on Ithaca, with an X-marks-the-spot on her little house with the blue shutters. I'd be there soon. I was on my way, and she knew nothing. What a moment it would be.

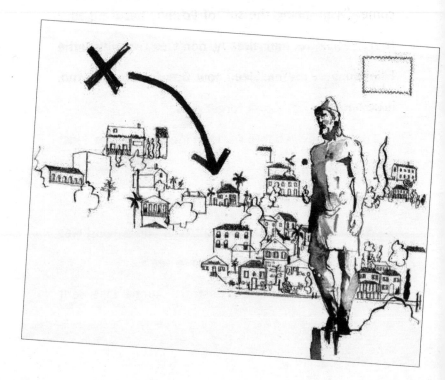

My Odyssey

I don't think I ever realised until now how unbelievably vast Australia is. It goes on and on, hours and hours of it. The sun's going down over Australia, over my childhood. Not sad any more. Excited. Got to try to get some sleep. Not going to be easy. Flight's bumpy, and the baby in the seat behind is cooing loudly. Still, I suppose cooing is better than crying.

Greece, here I come. Ithaca, here I come. Homer and Odysseus and Penelope, here I come. Proteus, here I come. (Well, being the son of Poseidon and a god, I think you know that already, don't you?) And Auntie Ellie too, here I come. Sleep now. Coo-coo-too-yoo-too, little baby.

4 May

I'm sitting in a café outside a bus station in Athens. I've got to catch the bus to a place in the Peloponnese called Kyllini, where they told me I can get a boat to Ithaca. Hope they're right. I've got to wait for five hours. So a good time to write my diary. It's as hot as Australia, but all the birds are different, no mynah birds, or ibis – bin chickens at home! – no galahs, and not a kangaroo or a koala in sight. I'm finding I can understand enough modern Greek to get by, from the few words Auntie Ellie taught me to speak, and through the Ancient Greek I learned at school. The modern does echo the ancient, and that helps.

When I landed a couple of days ago, I thought I'd spend some time in Athens before catching the ferry. Found a room above a bar near the Acropolis. Bit noisy, but the music down below was Greek and I loved it. I recognised the tune from *Zorba*. You hear it everywhere. I could see Auntie Ellie dancing as I listened. Walked a lot, ate kebabs and chips, and moussaka and chips, more than once. The moussaka reminded me of home, but Ma cooks it differently, better. I loved the bustle of the city, but hated the traffic. And there are too many tourists like me. Smelly, noisy – the traffic, I mean, not the tourists! I took my life in my hands

every time I crossed the road. Spent hours up at the Acropolis. Couldn't believe I was standing there, the place I'd read so much about, where democracy began in Ancient Greece.

Went to see a play on my first evening in Athens, in the open-air Ancient Greek theatre. It was *Antigone,* a play by Sophocles, a tragedy. I had read it before at school, but to see it on stage here in Athens with the Acropolis right there, maybe in the theatre where it was first performed over two thousand years before was amazing. I understood enough of it to be able to enjoy it, the Ancient Greek, and felt very pleased with myself about that.

I was surrounded by tourists, and I suddenly felt very proud to feel at least a bit Greek, not just a visitor. Because of this place, because people like Sophocles wrote a play like *Antigone*, because he and other great writers spoke out against tyranny, I can live in a place like Australia where we can speak our minds, be free, be who we want to be. And it's the same for Greeks here today, and for most of those people who were sitting all around me in that great and ancient theatre. The best night of my life. Now I really am in Greece, I know there will be many other best nights.

I would have stayed and stayed in Athens, but I want to get to Ithaca to see Auntie Ellie. I can't wait to see the look on her face when I turn up out of the blue. It's been five years since we last met. She might not even recognise me. I'll talk Australian – she will then. Not long now.

Think that's my bus. Better get moving. Rucksack's really heavy – always hate the thought of putting it on. Know what a tortoise feels like!

5 May

First sighting of Ithaca! Just a dark shadow on the horizon. One of the crew on the ferry just told me, pointing out to sea. 'Ithaca,' he said.

'Do you live there?' I asked him, in my best ancient and modern Greek. I was hoping he might know Auntie Ellie.

'No, no,' he replied. 'But Odysseus did. Homer did.'

'Penelope too,' I said. He laughed. I think he seemed pleased I knew.

Writing this up on deck. This is just how Odysseus must have seen it when he left to go to the Trojan Wars, and when he came home again ten years later, how Auntie Ellie saw it on the last leg of her trip home every time she came to visit us in Australia.

And there really are flying fish! Dozens of them,

flashing silver in the sun as they leap out of the water and fly, miraculously fast, skimming the surface before diving in again. Maybe some of them have come all the way from Australia, from the Yarra River. Maybe among them is the very one I saw all those years ago when I skipped school that day.

Only a couple of hours now till we get there, till I see Auntie Ellie again.

Dolphins! At least six of them, darting and diving and leaping through the waves alongside the boat. What a welcome! Flying fish and dolphins! Every one of them like a shining god, every one a Proteus maybe. Who knows? He knows, all the gods know I'm here, know I'm coming, coming home. That's what it feels like. I've lived almost all my life in amongst the stories of this place, and now I don't have to imagine it any more. I'm almost there, really there. I'll soon be where Odysseus lived, where Penelope wove her tapestry, and where the gods wove their story, just as they are weaving my story right now.

Evening of the same day

So difficult to write this because I know I will have to relive it as I tell it. And it'll make me sad all over again. But I must do it because it has happened. You can't unknow what you know. And there's no point in a diary if you can't tell it true. Take a deep breath, Nandi, and write.

Vathy looks like a lovely small town with its houses and restaurants gathered round a harbour full of yachts coming and going, some tied up on the quayside. Little it may be, compared to Melbourne, but I was told Vathy is the biggest town on the whole island of Ithaca.

I knew exactly where Auntie Ellie lives. I have her address, and at least three different postcards on my bedroom wall at home in Melbourne with her actual house in the picture, a small place right on the seafront with light blue shutters and a light blue door. It was the house where she was born, where she grew up. Each one of these postcards has an X-marks-the-spot on her house. And I had the last card she sent with me. She always told me that if ever I came I couldn't miss it. And she was right. I got off the bus, took one look across the harbour and there it was. Auntie Ellie's house, white and blue in the sunlight, just where X-marked-the-spot.

Heaving up my rucksack for the last time, I made my way round the harbour, past a supermarket and a few restaurants and cafés, mostly empty, tables and chairs waiting for evening customers. There were a few people about. I was already looking around for Auntie Ellie. Every time I saw an old lady – and some of them, like her, were dressed all in black too – I thought it might be her, which was silly, I know. It's just that with every step I took my heart was filled with such longing to see her again, to see the surprise on her face. As I walked towards the house, my rucksack wasn't heavy any more, my legs weren't tired. There was a spring in my step, joy in my heart.

I climbed the front step, took off my rucksack and knocked on the door.

No one answered. So I knocked again and waited a while. Nothing. I listened at the door, peered in at the window. No one was there. I tapped on the window and called her. I went round the back and looked in at a kitchen window. It was tidy inside, too tidy. There

were no plates out on the table, waiting to be washed up, no food left on the worktop, and nothing in the sink or on the draining board. Then I saw the photos on the fridge, some definitely of me, some of Ma and Papa, and a few postcards of wombats, and possums, and kangaroos that I knew I'd sent her. This was the right house, no mistake. But she wasn't here, and by the look of it she hadn't been here for some time.

A voice spoke from right behind me and made me jump. I turned round. It was a policeman. He spoke to me in English. 'She's not in,' he told me. 'She's gone.'

I thought I'd better explain myself. I told him I had come from Australia to see her, that I was a relative and she was my great-aunt. I asked when she would be back.

'Nobody knows,' he said, shrugging. 'She did not say. Nobody knows why she has gone, and nobody knows where she is. But she will be back. She promised Maria she'd be back – she had a postcard – and Elena always keeps her promises. And she always comes back. But when? Who knows?'

I tried to hide my disappointment. But the tears were coming anyway. I had to wipe them away.

'Australia? It is a very long

way you have come.' He was scrutinising me closely now. 'I think you are Nandi, no? From Australia, yes? Elena, she has many photos of you. You are family, no? She speaks of you many times. She always says one day you will come. So this is how I know you are Nandi. You have a room, somewhere to stay?' I shook my head. 'It is all right. My sister, Maria, she has a house a little way down the road. She is good friend to Elena, best friend. I will fix. You will stay there with her. Come, come.'

So that's where I am now, up in a little room overlooking the harbour, bed, chair and table by the window. I'm sitting at the table writing this. A wind has got up this evening, and the boats are rocking all along the quayside, their lights dancing. Everyone has been very kind: the policeman – Costas – and his sister Maria, who put her arm round me when I arrived and took me in at once. I was sure by now this must be the Maria we knew was looking after Auntie Ellie.

She gave me supper and told me I could stay as long

as I liked, that any family of Elena was family to them and to everyone on the island. I could not understand everything she said because her Greek was too fast and her English hardly sounded like English. But I understood enough to know that it is on account of Auntie Ellie that I am an honoured guest in her house, on the island, and more than welcome.

So I should be happy enough, but I'm not. I'm in Ithaca, aren't I? I have a place to sleep and kind people about me. But Auntie Ellie isn't here, and as far as I can tell they don't have a clue where she went or when she might be back.

And I have no idea what to do, what to think. Do I just wait and hope? Where are you, Auntie Ellie? Where have you gone? Why have you gone? When are you coming back? No one seems to know. Or, if they do, they're not telling me. All Maria and Costas said is that she had been seen early one morning a month or so ago by a fisherman, getting into the little boat that she keeps on a nearby beach – Dexa Beach they called it, I think. And no one has seen her since. Just that one postcard to Maria, that's all anyone has heard of her, so far as I can tell.

I'm going to find her. I must. But how? Where do I start? I can't think straight. I'm just too upset to write another word. Too sad to sleep.

6 May

On Dexa Beach. Morning

I came here because it was the only place I could think of to begin my search. This was where she was last seen a month or so ago. I had to start somewhere. And anyway Maria said it was the best beach on the whole island to go for a swim, that she swims here whenever she can, and Auntie Ellie did too, every day. Auntie Ellie swims like a fish. I remembered, from our trips with her to the beach in Australia, being amazed how far she swam and how fast. And swimming, Maria said, would make me feel better.

She's being really lovely with me, and she keeps saying over and over how much she loves Auntie Ellie, how much everyone on the island loves her and misses her. She tells me I mustn't worry, that she will be back, that she's gone off before a few times in the last year or two, and always come back safe and sound. She has no idea where Auntie Ellie went, only that it was important for her to go.

Maria works in the health centre in Vathy. You can see the kindness in her face. She mothers me, and I like that. I don't think she has children of her own. But I haven't asked.

Missing Ma and Papa. Texted them, telling them I'm fine. Which I am, sort of.

Maria is wrong about swimming making you feel better. I've been in the sea twice now, swum up and down the whole length of the beach, and I don't feel any better. The water is warm and clean and calm, and it's beautiful here and quiet. There's no one about on the beach except me. There are olive trees to shade you from the sun, and the high hills around shelter you from the wind. I can see a small island out in the bay. I want to swim out to it, and I will, one day I will. In any tourist brochure, they would call this place a paradise, and it truly is. But my sadness, my disappointment that Auntie Ellie is not here will not leave me. All I can think of is that about a month or so ago Auntie Ellie must have walked down over these pebbles, climbed into a boat probably at the end of that little jetty and vanished.

I've got a good place to write. I'm sitting on the beach, my back against a low wall, my knees drawn up in front of me.

I am looking out at the jetty and the sea, the mountain beyond, and behind me is a grove of gnarled olive trees. I've been trying to imagine Auntie Ellie here, swimming in the sea in her black dress and her black scarf.

A while ago, I closed my eyes tight shut, willing her to be here, swimming in the sea, when I opened them. She's not.

I don't know what happened, what came over me. I was just wondering what to write about next in my diary when I suddenly found myself talking out loud to Auntie Ellie, telling her I was here, that I'd been missing her so much, that I had come all the way from Australia to Ithaca to see her. I was begging her to come back home.

'It's me! It's Nandi!'

I wasn't just talking any more, I was calling out to her at the top of my voice.

'It's me, Auntie Ellie! Nandi! I know you're there, Auntie Ellie!'

I don't know how I knew it, but someone was there. I could feel it. Someone was listening. Then a voice – it sounded like a woman's voice. I looked around. There was no one on the beach but me. Yet I was quite sure someone had heard me, that someone had spoken. At once, I was hoping and believing it was Auntie Ellie. The voice seemed to be talking to me from the waves far out to sea, almost singing to me, and calling me by my name. It had to be her! Who else knew my name? Only Maria and she wasn't here. No one was. The voice was telling me that she was waiting for me out there, that I should go to the end of the jetty and look down into the water where the little black fish always like to gather, that she'd be waiting for me there.

I was confused. The voice was inside my head now, but it still came from far out to sea as well, and from behind me, from in me and all around me. I was surrounded by it. But I knew now that it wasn't Auntie Ellie, not a woman's voice either, not a human voice at all. I was finding it hard to hear what it was saying, because it was whispering and distant, as if wind and waves were singing to me in a hushed chorus. All I knew for sure was that this voice was calling me, beckoning me, and that whoever it was had heard me, could see me, knew who I was, knew my name.

I feel cold with fear. I don't want to go. But I know I have to.

I'm sitting here, writing, trying somehow to drive away my fear with words, to face it, to reason with it. I'm trying to summon up the courage of Odysseus as he confronted the monsters on his travels, and the strength of Penelope as she faced up to her bullying suitors.

That singing, whispering voice, out there and in my head, scares me silly, but I know I have to do what it says. I have to walk down to the end of the jetty and swim again. I have to dive down into the shoals of little black fish, come up, and the voice will be there. I know it's the only way I'll find Auntie Ellie. That's what the voice is telling me. Odysseus and Penelope will be by my side, holding my hand. I'll go. I'm going. I'm going.

Same evening. My room in Vathy. Writing my diary in bed

Here's how the happening happened.

I don't remember walking back to Maria's house, only that I was shivering with cold when I got there. She made me stand under a hot shower until I had warmed all the cold out of me, then rubbed me dry and put me into bed under two duvets.

I've just read the last entry in my diary. It helped me to begin writing this. I have to get it down while it's still clear in my head.

Maria brought me up soup, hot lemony *avgolemono* soup, like Ma makes sometimes at home, and bread. She sat on the bed, both of us in silence. She reached out from time to time to touch my forehead and my cheek gently with the back of her hand. After I finished my soup, I lay back on the pillows and closed my eyes.

'Are you all right, Nandi?' she asked me then. 'Do you want to phone your mother?'

I shook my head.

I didn't want to speak to Ma or Papa. How could I tell them? What can I tell them? I'm still trying to believe it myself, still trying to work out whether I might be imagining the whole thing. Maybe I just fainted or something, and it's all a dream I had while I was unconscious. Or I'm ill, going mad in the head, seeing and hearing things that weren't there, that didn't happen.

I could tell Maria, but I don't know her well enough. Auntie Ellie is the only one I want to tell, but she's not here. Please let it all be true, a true happening. Please let me not be ill or mad in the head. Please.

Maria's gone downstairs now. As I'm writing this,

I can hear her speaking to Costas. They're talking in hushed voices and in Greek, so I can't understand much of what they're saying.

I'm going to write it all out, just as I remember it happening. Then I'll read it and decide if I believe it myself. If I do, then maybe I'll tell Maria, and see what she says. She's a nurse: she'll know if I'm ill, if I've been hearing and seeing things that aren't there.

Remember, Nandi. Remember. Write it down. Tell it just as it happened and you might believe it did.

I remember walking to the end of the jetty, and the voice still whispering to me. I remember how the stones in the concrete were so sharp they hurt the soles of my feet. I was sitting on the end of the jetty, paddling my feet in the water to make them feel better, wriggling my toes, when I saw him rise up out of the water right beside my feet.

I thought at first he was just an ordinary fish, much bigger than the little black ones that were always darting around the jetty, that liked to nibble my feet. But when I looked more closely I could see this was a different sort of fish altogether, that he was struggling to stay afloat, dying probably. He was bigger than any fish I'd seen anywhere around here, silvery, with a forked tail, and he shone in the sea. He had strange-looking fins as long as wings that were hanging down beside and beneath him. I felt he wanted to fly, to get out of the water and fly, but he couldn't.

A flying fish! It was a flying fish. It had to be.

I let myself down into the water. I was just about in my depth. I was nervous about doing it, but I knew I had to try to save this creature. I cupped my hands underneath him and lifted him gently out. He was not easy to hold. I could feel the strength in his wings. He was longing to fly, but hadn't the strength to do it. Not yet.

I remembered then how, back home in Melbourne, a little bird, a robin, had flown one morning into the window of our sitting room. I'd heard a thud against the glass, gone out and seen it lying there, either stunned or already dead, picked him up, felt the tiny heart beating, and just stood there cupping him, and hoping he would revive enough to fly again. And he had.

That's what I did with the flying fish. I stood there in the sea and held him and held him and hoped and hoped.

And then I remembered so clearly the flying fish I had seen that day as I was walking along the banks of the Yarra River, back in Melbourne. That one was silver, and with a forked tail. This one was silver with a forked tail. It could have been any of thousands, millions of flying fish. I knew that. But at that moment I was quite sure, I *am* quite sure, beyond any doubt, that I was holding in my hands the very same flying fish, that somehow we were meant to meet again here on this beach in Ithaca.

I wanted to calm him, to reassure him. So I spoke to him very softly, stroking the crown of his head with my thumb. I felt him go limp in my hands. I thought he was dead. Then his eyes opened and he looked up at me steadily, meaningfully. Our eyes met. These were not the eyes of a fish. These were eyes that were looking deep into mine, that understood. He had a strange face, like a fishy old man with whiskers. I was still worried he might be dying. Now, as I stroked him, his eyes opened wider and his mouth moved. And he spoke. He spoke. It was just a moan at first, like the sound of a sad frog singing softly. Then he was speaking to me, in a whisper, in the same faraway singing whisper I had heard before. But he wasn't far away: he was cupped in my hands.

I won't pretend I remember every word he said. But I do remember what he told me, and in detail.

'You are Nandi,' he began. 'I am Proteus. I am the son of the sea god Poseidon, and I can be whoever I wish to be. As you see, if I wish to be a flying fish, I am. If I wish to be a dolphin, I am. If I wish to be a crab or a whale, I am. I came to see you once before. I was a flying fish then too, if you remember. I was in a river that flows from Australia into the Southern Ocean. I knew you would be there. I saw you; you saw me. You are here now, Nandi, because I wanted you to come, and because you wanted to visit your Auntie Ellie. It is what we gods do. We fulfil wishes when we feel like it. And I felt like it.

'Some of us, when we are angry, can make the earth tremble and the seas flood. But we do not make the world as it is. People do that. People do what they wish to do: great and good things, cruel and terrible things. And we gods are like people, not always wise. We can be kind and loving one moment, vengeful and jealous the next. But we are powerful. We can help and encourage and arrange happenings – great and good happenings, cruel and terrible happenings. We can make wishes and dreams come true, or not. As we wish. Call us dream-makers, dream-fakers, dream-breakers. We are gods. We do what we please.

'But enough of me –' his whispering was weaker now – 'enough of gods. I wanted to make your wish to come to Ithaca happen. I wanted you to find your Auntie Ellie, and I very nearly did, but not quite. I have brought you all this way, from the Yarra River – where I first put the thought into your head, if you remember – to Ithaca, but you came too late. She has gone. I have heard your cries and your tears, and have decided I should tell you all about your Auntie Ellie. It might help explain why she is not here, why she has left. She has had a long life, so it will be a long story.'

I had to bend closer to hear his husky whispering now.

'She may seem to you like a little old Greek lady, just your kindly old auntie. Kindly she certainly is, but she is much more than that. I have noticed, Nandi, how much you admire your Ancient Greek heroes, especially Odysseus and Penelope. I knew them well. We gods live for ever, and know and have known everything and everyone we want to know. We see the whole world in the blink of an eye, hear and remember every spoken word. We know past and future; we help arrange it, help it all happen.

'I am here to tell you something you do not know, and that you need to know. That your aunt is a great hero, more heroic than any sword-wielding, spear-throwing warrior of Ancient Greece, far braver than great Odysseus and even your beloved Penelope. Auntie Ellie is a modern Greek hero, a hero of today and yesterday and tomorrow, which, as you will soon discover, is why you do not find her here.'

His whispering seemed to be fading away fast.

'That is all I will tell you for now, Nandi. Come again tomorrow. Same place, same time, as the sun goes over the hill, when there are few people about so we can talk in private. Let me go now. I must fly. I must swim. I like being a flying fish – flying, swimming, the best of all worlds – but I cannot stay too long out of the water.'

I opened my hands, held him up, and away he flew, skimming low over the sea, then diving in, disappearing and leaving me alone and cold in the water.

7 May

Late morning

I've been in a daze since yesterday evening, unable to think of anything but that singing, whispering voice, that silver flying fish looking up at me from my cupped hands. Ever since I woke up, I've been trying to convince myself that none of it could have taken place, that it must have been imagined. Then I read my diary and I know for sure the happening really happened. But I only have to think about it and I still can't believe it.

I've just texted home, telling Ma and Papa that I'm fine, that all is well. I knew they'd be worrying. I told them what I knew they wanted to hear, and left out the bit about meeting up with Proteus in the guise of a talking flying fish!

Sleeping was difficult last night, what with my mind whirring, spinning with doubt and excitement. And there's a mosquito bite on my ankle that is driving me mad. Maria put some cream on it. I think from the way she looks at me that she knows something has happened. She's very instinctive, or is it intuitive? I so want to tell her everything, but I can't. Why should she believe it when I'm struggling to believe it myself? She'd think I'd been seeing things, that I'd had too much sun or something.

To pass the time this morning, I've been exploring, walking up in the valley behind Dexa Beach. There are olive trees everywhere and beehives, and sheep too, mostly higher up on the hills. You can't see them often, but you can hear them bleating, and you can hear their bells all the time. I love this place. I'm calling it the Valley of the Bells. I've climbed up through the olive grove to the highest hill and sat down on a rock at the top to write this. Maybe Homer sat on this very rock. Maybe he saw Odysseus walking up out of the waves, saw him changing into beggar's clothes to disguise himself, and then walking homewards up the beach towards his palace, after the Trojan War and his ten years of journeying, longing to see his Penelope.

I'm looking down on Dexa Beach right now from my writing rock, the sheep all around me bleating, bells tinkling, jangling. I can see the jetty. Same time, same place, the flying fish said yesterday. I'll be there. Not scared any more. There's only one thing that bothers me now, and that's if Proteus doesn't come back. If he's not there this evening when I go down to the beach, then it'll mean that I was hearing voices that weren't there, seeing things that weren't there. And that does worry me.

I so want him to be there, so want it all to have been true and not imagined. And I so want to hear more about Auntie Ellie. Hard to think of her as a hero. She's nice old Auntie Ellie to me, just about my favourite person in all the world. But a hero?

The sheep are getting very friendly. I think they like me being up here with them, or maybe it's my hummus sandwich they're after. I love the sound of their bells. They're a bit smelly, these sheep, but I won't tell them that. Come to think of it, I reckon they're goats not sheep. Goats are properly smelly. Yep, these are definitely goats.

Past seven o'clock already. Time flies when you're writing. I'll go down to the beach, have a quick swim, and be at the end of the jetty about the same time as yesterday. There's a few people down there swimming, more than yesterday, but they'll be gone soon.

Hadn't noticed it before. I can see a huge yellow house just above the beach that's seen better days. It must have been a grand place once. No one living there now by the looks of it. Deserted. All grown over.

Wonder who lived there. Sad to see. I've noticed quite a few abandoned-looking houses on the island, only stone walls left standing. This one isn't in ruins, and it's the biggest by far.

Better get going. Sun's going down behind the hill. I think this Valley of the Bells is the most beautiful, most peaceful place. Olive trees everywhere. There's a gentle wind in the trees, and I think I hear cicadas. I feel I belong here.

Same evening. In a café by the port. Vathy

Lots to report. Lots to take in. Lots to write.

I had a swim, accompanied by my escort of little black fish. I stopped swimming from time to time and stood there, looking all around for any sign of the flying fish above or below the water. I expected him any time. There was still one family with lots of children at the far end of the beach, but they were packing up to go. I swam over to the jetty, sat on the end of it as I had before, my legs dangling. The little black fish were around my feet at once, nibbling, tickling me. They were company, calming me as I waited.

He wasn't long in coming. He came flying towards me, fast and low, a flash of silver in the evening sun, then diving down into the sea nearby, scattering all the little black fish, before surfacing right under my feet at the end of the jetty. I let myself down into the water beside him.

'Shall I pick you up?' I asked him.

'Why not?' he replied. So, cupping my hands, I lifted him carefully out of the water just as I had before, and held him, the water dripping through my fingers. I felt his wings go limp as he relaxed in my hands.

We looked at one another for a few moments in silence. I thought of saying hello, but it seemed just not the right way to speak to either a flying fish or a god. So I said the first thing that came into my head.

'Auntie Ellie, she still hasn't come back.'

'There'll be a reason for that, Nandi,' he whispered. 'She'll be busy. But she'll come when she can, when she's ready. Soon, you'll see.'

There was another long silence between us. 'I'm glad

you came,' I told him, 'because now I can believe you really were here yesterday, that I didn't dream you, that I'm not seeing things that aren't there, that I'm not mad. I'm not dreaming you now, am I?'

'You may be,' he whispered. 'Who knows where dreams end and reality begins, or if they are not one and the same?'

'I thought gods knew the answers to all those sort of questions,' I said.

He laughed then. I had not heard him laugh before. It was a whispery sort of chortling.

'We think we do. I told you, we are quite like people. Some of us gods think we know everything. Not true for people, not true for gods. But no more of this philosophising. I haven't the time. As you saw yesterday, I tire quickly when I'm out of the water for too long. I must get on and tell you more about your Auntie Ellie, who is, as you will hear, as great a Greek hero as any of the Ancients.'

And this is what he told me, not quite word for word, but as near to that as I can remember.

'You must think of your Auntie Ellie differently now, Nandi,' he went on, 'and try to imagine her as she was when I first saw her, over eighty years ago, as a little girl of seven or eight maybe, her father a fisherman, and with no mother. She had a brother, Manos, two years younger than she was. But they had no mother. She had died when they were little. She was mother and sister to that boy. As she grew up, she was the little mother, looking after father and brother alike, and the bees and the goats and the olive trees too. She kept the house, fed the animals, cooked the food, fetched the water. But, whenever she could be, she was out fishing with her father, little Manos fishing too, hunkering down out of the wind at the bottom of the boat. She learned to handle a boat as well as any man on the island, as easy at sea, in the water, as she was on dry land. There was no time for school. She taught herself everything she knew. The sea and the island and her family and her animals were her teachers and her classroom.

'Then, a long time ago now, when Elena – your Auntie Ellie as you think of her – was still very young, Greece was attacked and invaded by the Italians. These islands have been occupied many times over the centuries. I've seen them all come and go, these invaders. Pirates came and went, burning, looting. The Venetians came, the Turks, the French, the British, and then the Italians. But the worst of them all, the cruellest, were the Germans, the Nazis. They came after the Italians. No one liked the Italians. Who likes an occupier, an invader? But the Nazis did a lot more than occupy and invade Ithaca, and Kefallonia too, the island across the water. They killed and murdered; they burned whole villages to the ground.

'This was the worst war the world had ever known. You call it the Second World War. The Nazis, who by now had occupied all of Greece, all the islands too, took whatever they wanted: food, machinery, petrol. Everywhere the people went hungry. The invaders arrested and took away anyone that they didn't like and shot anyone who resisted. This all happened when Elena was just eighteen, and Manos was sixteen, and a fisherman now like his father.

'Then one night Manos stole away from the house without telling his father or sister because he knew they would try to stop him. With two of his fishermen friends, they went over the water to Kefallonia, to join the resistance fighters there, the partisans. His bed was empty in the morning. Elena knew where he had gone – he had been determined to go over and join the fight there ever since the occupiers had come. She had told him again and again that he was too young. But he would not listen. He was young, young and brave. They all were.

'The next night, under cover of darkness, not telling her father, Elena rowed across to Kefallonia to find Manos and bring him back. It took some days for her to find him – moving around the island was difficult and dangerous. She found one or two people there who knew her father and Manos, and they helped her. They warned her that there were German soldiers everywhere, with their guns and their tanks. They told her never to go near the villages and towns, because that's where the soldiers were garrisoned.

'"You must go to the hills," they told her. "That's where the partisan fighters are. You'll be safer up there, and that's where you'll find Manos." And that's where they took her.

'She found him in the end, with his friends, hiding away in a cave deep in the hills.

'She tried to persuade him to come home, but it was no good. She could see Manos was not her little brother any more, but a young man who was as determined as all his comrades to stay and fight. So she decided she had to do the same, so she could be with him. And she soon found herself looking after all his friends too. She f etched food for them from the farms down in the valleys, carried guns and ammunition for them, took messages to other groups all over the island. Elena knew how dangerous it was, that she would be shot if she was caught. But it was the same for Manos, for all of them.

'She had seen the burnt-out villages with her own eyes, had been told of atrocities and massacres, witnessed executions, seen the freshly dug graves. All Elena knew was that the enemy had to be driven into the sea, that she had no choice but to stay and fight with Manos and his friends. One of them, Manos's best friend, was a young man called Alexis, who from the first moment she saw him looked like a Greek god to her. We gods can sometimes look like gods, you know.'

'Alexis?' I remembered the name at once. 'I think maybe I know about this Alexis,' I told him. 'They were married, weren't they? My ma said . . .' But I stopped then. I had interrupted Proteus and suddenly realised I'd upset him. He was looking up at me, reproaching me with his unblinking eyes.

For a while, he stayed there, lying in my hands, staring at me, silent, sullen even. Then he said: 'Who is telling this story, your ma or me? I have flown and swum halfway round the globe to be with you, to tell you Elena's story.

Do you want me to go on or don't you? Gods do not like to be interrupted – remember that.'

'I'm sorry,' I said hastily. 'Please.'

'No more today,' he whispered, shifting in my hands. I could feel his wings wanting to fly, that he was wanting to be gone. 'Tomorrow. I'm tired now. I find it sometimes hard to talk, especially when there is sadness. And with war there is always sadness. Tomorrow, same time, same place, and I'll tell you all about Alexis, just so long as you don't interrupt. I like Alexis. You will like Alexis. Elena loved Alexis. Lift me now. I have to go.'

As I've been writing this up in my room, I keep thinking long and hard about asking Maria. She would know more. After everything Proteus told me today, I'm so wanting to find out all I can, all she can tell me about Alexis and Auntie Ellie, about how they met, and what had happened to him. I know he died young, that Auntie Ellie has been alone most of her long life.

Mama told me that much. But Maria is working late, and Costas is on duty.

I'm sitting up in bed, writing away, listening to the sea lapping against the harbour wall, and the clapping of the rigging in yacht masts in the breeze. And I keep hoping against hope the two of them, Auntie Ellie and Alexis, had at least some years of happiness together. I'll know soon enough.

Tomorrow. And tomorrow is always another day, another story. This time tomorrow I'll be sitting here, writing down in this diary whatever it will be that my Proteus, my flying fish, has told me. I'll know all about Alexis who had looked to my Auntie Ellie, 'from the first moment she saw him,' as Proteus had told me, 'like a god.'

8 May

Sitting on the seawall in Vathy under a streetlamp, the sea darkening

Just enough light to write by. I've got Homer on my mind. As the sun goes down here on Ithaca, I realise Homer was not simply using poetic licence when he called it 'a wine-dark sea'. There is a moment on Ithaca, when the last of the sun catches the ripple of the waves, when these Ionian waters do become a sea of wine, dark red wine.

This was my day. To pass the time, to make it go more quickly before our meeting at the end of the jetty in the evening, I took a bus this morning and went to see Homer's house, high on a hillside at the other end of the island. Sitting in amongst the scattered stones of his house, in the shade of ancient olive trees, I could look out to sea and be where he sat, for a while, where he wrote the *Odyssey* and the *Iliad*. I had the lunch Maria had given me – bread and tomato and feta cheese and olives – much the same lunch as Homer would very likely have eaten all those thousands of years ago. I had grazing goats all around me, their smell too – their bells sounding in the warmth of the air.

But I could not think of Odysseus coming home, or of Penelope waiting for him, longing for him to be with her again. I knew their story. The thought in my head was of another couple whose story I still didn't know, but that I was going to find out about soon enough.

I got a lucky lift back to Dexa Beach on the back of a scooter. I had to cling on tight and close my eyes more than once or twice going round corners, dodging wandering sheep. My driver, who was not at all talkative, told me in English that he had grown up in Vathy, and asked why I had come to Ithaca. Was it because of Odysseus? I said it was because of Elena who was my Auntie Ellie. Once he knew that, he treated me not like a tourist at all, but more like an old friend.

He talked non-stop then. His English wasn't good, but I could understand enough to know that he, like everyone else, thought the world of Auntie Ellie. He called her 'the Queen of Ithaca' and said that, if I was from her family, then I was a cousin of everyone on the island, including him.

I arrived at Dexa Beach dusty and shaken, but basking in the warmth of his welcome, with a new sense that I belonged in this place as much if not more than I had ever belonged in Melbourne.

The beach was deserted, except for a boy sitting inconveniently at the end of my jetty, swinging his legs in the water. He heard me coming and turned round. He looked English. He was wearing a red Manchester United baseball cap.

'The black fish,' he said, giggling. 'They tickle.'

'They can bite too,' I told him. I felt a bit mean saying that, but it did the trick.

He got up quite fast and left me there on my own, which was, of course, what I wanted. I sat down in his place and waited. When the little black fish suddenly swarmed and swam away, I knew my flying fish was coming. And then, moments later, there he was, looking up at me. I slipped myself down into the water gently, held my cupped hands out to him, and let him swim on to them, rest his fins and settle.

'I was going to tell you about Alexis, wasn't I?' he began, his singsong whispering softer than before, almost as if he was reluctant to say what he was going to have to tell me. 'Alexis and Elena met on Kefallonia, in a village high in the mountains. They met because they were meant to meet. It was a moonlit night. Alexis was hiding away in his grandmother's house, looking after her as best he could. She had not been well. He was her only grandson, and she had brought him up as a child. The two were best friends in the world, as often grandmother and grandson are.

'Alexis knew it was dangerous to stay for too long, but he could not bring himself to leave her. Word had reached the partisans hidden in their mountain cave that the Nazis were going to be searching the village where she lived, and Manos had volunteered to warn Alexis, and bring him back up the mountain to the safety of their hideaway. Elena insisted on going with them.

'The village was silent and sleeping. Manos knew the house. He'd been there before. He stood in the street and hooted like an owl, quietly, two hoots and a half, a signal known to partisan fighters needing to find each other at night. After some moments, an upstairs window opened. Alexis looked out and saw him, saw Elena too. And she saw Alexis. You could say the moonlight did the rest. And the gods.

'It happens in peace; it happens in war. It happens with people; it happens with gods. The two of them were beautiful to one another, at once dear to one another, and, in the days and weeks and months that followed, the love between them grew, even living as they were, hidden away in a cave, even thinking every day might be their last. They were lovers, sharing their lives with the best of friends, comrades fighting side by side for democracy and freedom, for their islands and for the country so dear to their hearts. They were a band of brothers and sisters. They were together.

'They talked more in those few short months than most couples talk in a lifetime. Deep down, they both knew they might not have that lifetime, but they made plans for it anyway, dreamed it, hoped for it, lived for it. They would take Alexis's grandmother, who was all the family he had on Kefallonia, back to Ithaca, and live there in Elena's home, with Manos and her father. They would have children, lots of children. They would grow olives, keep sheep and goats, and hens. They would have the family boat, and would all go fishing, and the children would be shepherds, and would help with the olive harvest, and play on the beach, and swim in the sea, and there would be blessed peace at last, and freedom to enjoy it.

'But first the peace had to be fought for. Without peace, they knew all their dreams would come to nothing. So the resistance and the fighting went on. There were never enough fighters, never enough arms or ammunition, never enough food. There were times when the struggle seemed hopeless. They lost friends, good and dear friends, brave friends. But they never gave up hope.

'Then one day Manos was wounded during a skirmish, a firefight, in the hills. It was a muddle of a battle, as most battles are. The resistance fighters happened by accident on a German patrol in a valley. The Germans were as surprised as they were. Bullets went flying everywhere. The Germans ran away, the partisans ran away, except for Manos who couldn't run. He had a bullet wound in his foot.

'Alexis carried him all the way back up to the cave. To go down into a town to see a doctor was too risky. There were Germans everywhere there. Elena knew it would be safer to take Manos to their uncle, the island doctor on Ithaca. He would look after him, and anyway it was safer on Ithaca. There weren't so many Germans over on Ithaca. There was no time to lose. The wound was deep, and there was always the risk of infection and gangrene. They had to get Manos to Ithaca as quickly as they could.

'So Alexis carried him on his shoulders all the way back down to the coast. But, when they got there, they could not find a boat. Elena decided there was only one thing to do. Alexis would stay by the seashore, and look after Manos, while she swam over to Ithaca to find her father. They would bring his fishing boat over, pick up Alexis and Manos, and take them back to Ithaca.

'Alexis said he should go, that he was the stronger swimmer. They had their first argument on that beach.

'Elena wouldn't listen to him. "You've just carried Manos all the way down the mountain," she insisted. "You're exhausted. And anyway I'm a better swimmer. You stay with him. I'm going. I'll be back soon." And, with that, Elena just walked off into the sea. So that's what happened, Nandi. Elena, your Auntie Ellie, just

walked down into the moonlit sea, and swam all the way across to Ithaca. And no waters around Ithaca are more treacherous than that channel.

'I was there all the way to witness it, Nandi. I swam beside her, leaping up out of the sea from time to time so that she could see me flying ahead of her, like a silver

arrow in the moonlight pointing out the best and safest way across. I know the pull of the currents out there. I've felt those angry, wind-whipped waves. I may have helped guide her, but Elena swam that treacherous channel herself, never stopping, not for one moment. Yes, I willed her on, but she had willpower enough of her own. Nothing was going to stop her reaching the shore, not the waves, not the currents, not the cold, not her tiring arms, not her cramping legs. And reach it she did.

'She did not stop to rest even then. As soon as her feet touched the sand, she was running. She ran up the beach, over the hills, out and down into the town to fetch her father and the fishing boat. And back they came that same night to pick up Alexis and Manos, waiting for them on the shore of Kefallonia. Under cover of the last of the night, the moon hidden now, they reached Ithaca and safety. I swam all the way back with them, leaping for joy in the wake of their boat.'

I remember, as he was telling me all this, how I was

struggling to contain my feelings. This was my Auntie Ellie! My Auntie Ellie had done this! But I didn't want to hear more. I knew I was about to be deeply saddened. I knew already that she and Alexis did not have long together, that he had died young. Suddenly I didn't want to hear how it was going to happen.

'Of course, there were Nazis too on Ithaca, not nearly so many, but they still had to be careful,' Proteus went on, his whispering weaker by now. 'There's a big yellow house just behind this beach. It belonged to Elena's uncle, the doctor. It's well hidden away, a huge house in the valley with olive and cypress trees all around.

It's still there. You may have noticed it. There the doctor looked after Manos; here Elena, Alexis and Manos hid away. His wound took a long while to heal. The ankle bone had been shattered. Manos never walked again afterwards without a limp. But the good doctor had saved his leg, saved his life.

'The first proper walk Manos took when he was well enough was up to the chapel under the high hill on the Pisaetos road, to be with Elena and Alexis on the day they were married. Manos insisted on going, limping all the way. He was Alexis's best man. The whole island came. It was, many people say, the only happy day on the island during the long months and years of occupation. Alexis picked some purple gladioli from the roadside as they walked down the hill into Vathy town afterwards, and gave them to Elena. It was a moment she never forgot.

'The two of them had five weeks together in the doctor's house, that's all. And Manos was with them much of the time. The three musketeers, they called themselves. All for one and one for all. To begin with, no one spoke of going back over to Kefallonia to rejoin the fight. But, as time went by, and the more they talked of it, the more Elena realised that Alexis would soon have to leave, that their partisan friends carrying on the struggle in the hills of Kefallonia needed all the help they could get.

'But Elena knew also that she had to stay and look after Manos, who was still weak from his wound, and her father too was not well. Like so many, after all the long years of hunger, he was weakened and frail. Hunger and illness were everywhere now, all over the island. The best of the food, the fish, the meat, the vegetables – and there was little enough of it anyway – the Nazi occupiers always took for themselves. Elena had no choice. She could not leave her family. She tried all she could to persuade Alexis not to go, but she knew it was hopeless.

'So one night she took Alexis back across the sea to Kefallonia in the fishing boat. They parted on the beach, the two of them holding on to one another, never wanting to let go. They told each other they would be together again, and very soon, when peace came. Then they would start their lives again, have their own children, and live out their dreams. They promised one another they would make it happen.

'They were full of sadness at that moment, but full of hope too. They knew the war was coming to an end, that the invaders would soon be gone and all of Greece would be free again. Alexis stood on the beach and watched the boat slip away into the darkness. And Elena watched him fade away and become part of the shore.

'She never saw him again. Just a few weeks after, Alexis and some of his comrades were betrayed. They were discovered in their cave in the hills, and died fighting. Alexis was buried on Kefallonia. On the anniversary of her wedding day every year, Elena always goes over there to put Alexis's favourite flowers on his grave: purple gladioli. She has never missed an anniversary in all these years, not once.'

I think Proteus must have seen the tears in my eyes. I felt him brushing his wings up against my fingers, stroking me to comfort me, as I had once stroked him.

He just said: 'Till tomorrow, same place, Nandi, as the sun goes down over the hill.'

I opened my hands and let him fly.

'I'll be here,' I told him.

I still have tears in my eyes now as I'm writing this. I'm thinking that Auntie Ellie is almost becoming Elena to me now, not just my lovely old, dear old Auntie Ellie. And I'm thinking – and saying it out loud as I am writing: 'Please come home, Elena. Please, Auntie Ellie.'

It just occurred to me that thinking it and saying it and willing it are not enough. Somehow I have to help make it happen, make her come home. There has to be a way. Has to be.

9 May

Morning in my room

Yesterday evening, walking back along the road into Vathy, my head and heart were still full of the story of Elena and Alexis. All round the harbour the lights were glittering, and people were already out in the streets for their evening stroll. I was hoping against hope that Auntie Ellie might have come back, that there would be lights on in her house, that she would be there. But, as I came closer, I could see across the harbour that her windows were still dark.

As I walked towards Maria's house, I saw she was outside in the street, talking to her brother, Costas. He wasn't in his police uniform. Both were clearly dressed up to go out, and they also seemed to be waiting for me, I thought. They looked relieved to see me, almost as if they'd been wondering where I was, and I was late. They didn't let me go into the house, but, taking an arm each, turned me round and walked me straight down the street and, without a word of explanation, led me into a restaurant that was full of people, all smiling at me as I came in, and clapping.

I had no idea what was going on, but I was about to find out. Maria waved them all to silence. She spoke in Greek, then a bit in English, then Greek again. I understood some of it, but not all.

I think she said something like: 'This is Nandi – some of you have met her already – Elena's great-niece from Australia. We all recognise her from the photos Elena shows us, don't we? Now, for reasons we don't know, Elena is not here. She will be back soon. Whenever she goes off on her travels, she always comes back sooner or later, doesn't she? And always in time for her wedding-anniversary trip to take flowers to her beloved Alexis on Kefallonia. We know she never misses that – we know our Elena. We have not seen her for a while now, and we've been missing her already. But Nandi has not seen her for five years, and she has come all the way to Ithaca from Australia to visit her. Elena is like family to everyone on this island . . .' They all clapped again at this. 'So Nandi is family too. And, when family comes to visit on Ithaca, we have a welcoming party, don't we?'

It was such a surprise, such an evening. I had never felt so welcome, or so Greek, in all my life. They all spoke too fast, and the noise around the table was too loud, so I could understand very little. We had fish soup from a great tureen in the middle of the table, full of all sorts of fish – no flying fish, I'm glad to say! – lovely crusty bread, and afterwards cheese, and wine, and grapes, watermelon, and *baclava* too, just like we have at home in Melbourne, dripping with honey.

There was music and dancing. And I recognised so many of Auntie Ellie's favourite tunes and songs, 'Zorba's Dance' amongst them.

'Mikis Theodorakis!' I said, remembering.

That impressed them, and they were very impressed with my Greek dancing too, mostly taught by Auntie Ellie, of course. To be dancing like this in Ithaca with my Greek 'family' filled me with such happiness. Only Auntie Ellie was missing. If she'd been there, I was thinking, if Elena had been there with us all, it would have been perfect.

But then I thought that she was there, in spirit. These people love and honour her. But how much did they know about her swim, her great and heroic swim? No one had spoken of it. In Australia, we had known so little of her life, so little of who she was, what she had done. These people must know her so much better, maybe all about her. However much they knew, or how little, this party was for her in her absence as much as it was for me.

I lay in bed last night, wondering if I should ask Maria now what she knew about Elena and Alexis, and about the years of occupation, about why there were so many ruined houses on the island. And I wanted to know who lived now in the big yellow house in the Valley of the Bells, where the doctor had lived, where they had looked after Manos. And where was the church where Elena and Alexis had been married? I had so many questions whirring round my mind that I did not sleep well at all. Or maybe it was the thunderstorm crashing round the harbour outside my window.

Morning now. Storm over. I have a lot to do, a whole lot to discover.

Evening of the same day. Back in my room

I have already found the answers to two of my questions without ever having to ask them. Proteus seems to know what I want to know before I ask. Well, he is a god – why wouldn't he?

The same family as yesterday did not stay so long down on the beach, perhaps because there was still thunder in the air, and the wind was getting up. It didn't seem to bother my flying fish. He was waiting for me this time. I didn't realise it at first. I was sitting waiting for him at the end of the jetty when I looked down and saw him lying there on the seabed, his wings or elongated fins outstretched – still not sure whether they are fins or wings – and the little black fish swimming all round him. He rose up through them and hung there in the water, waiting to be picked up.

As soon as I was holding him, he began talking in his mellifluous, whispering voice. 'Good party? You dance well, Nandi, but not as well as Elena. She danced wonderfully at her wedding, you know. Alexis sat and watched, entranced. And, just in case you were wondering after we met yesterday, and you want to find the chapel where they married all those years ago, it's on the road out past this beach, and towards the port of Pisaetos, on the right-hand side, under the high hill. You can walk there easily. There are olive trees all around, growing in amongst the ruins from ancient times, and goats wandering about as if they own the place, which, of course, they think they do. I was a goat that day, I was there – I told you, I am Proteus. I can be what I like. So I know goats for what they are. Smelly. I am smelly when I am a goat!

'Let me tell you about ruins, Nandi. Ithaca is an

island of ruins. Those ruins by the chapel under the hill, Homer's house, the palace of Odysseus and Penelope? All ruins. Not much left, of course, of any of them, but enough to know they were there. They used to be palaces and houses, whole towns and villages too. I know. I've seen buildings go up, and I've seen them come down. I've been around a long, long time, Nandi. An island of ruins, but it's still going, still a living place.

'But I need to tell you about ruins from more modern times, about Elena and the ruins of Ithaca. When her uncle, the doctor, died some years after the Nazi invaders were driven out, after that terrible war was over, he left that big yellow house in the valley to Elena. Soon after, her father died too, and so eventually she was living there with her brother Manos – who is your grandfather, of course – who suffered long after the war with his wound, and needed looking after. She kept bees and goats and sheep on the hillside, made cheese and honey, tended her olive trees and her vegetables.

And she went fishing too with Manos.

'In time, Manos found himself a wife. Zita was a girl from the village of Stavros. They went to live there in her family home, where he became a carpenter – he was always good with his hands, a practical sort of person. They soon had a son . . . yes, your papa.

'Elena, alone in the big house now, always called it Alexis's House, and everyone knew why. It was well known by now, across the whole island, how brave she and her brother and Alexis, the three musketeers (they were sometimes called), had been during the years of occupation. She was much loved and respected all over the island. They knew why she often seemed sad, how much – even all those years later – she wanted to be with Alexis. She liked just to keep herself to herself, and they all knew why. She swam here from this beach alone every day and in time it became known to many as 'Elena's beach'. It was then she began to look after it, picking up anything washed up on the shore, plastic, paper, bottles, tins. Every day after she swam, she would walk up and down the beach, leaving it clean, leaving it as it should be.'

I had to bend down close to him now to hear his whispers.

'I don't like to remember, or to speak of what I must now tell you. This island had suffered enough. Elena had suffered enough.'

He did not seem to want to go on, but he did.

'It was a lunchtime in the summer of 1953. Many were inside their houses. They were used to earth tremors – they happen often enough here and still do. But on this ordinary summer's day there came a great earthquake, and the earth shook with a terrible thunder, and the sky itself seemed to tremble, and the island was, in a few violent minutes, tumbled into ruins. Hardly a building was left standing in Vathy. And it was the same everywhere, all over Kefallonia too. Hundreds were buried in the rubble of their houses. There was fire and smoke everywhere.'

I had forgotten until now about the earthquake. Papa had told me of it, that he had no memories of it himself, how he was only little when it happened. But I remembered now that this was why they had left. This was the earthquake that had destroyed their house, that had forced his father to go to Australia, the earthquake that had made me Australian.

Proteus was telling me, whispering it to me. 'Elena was out in the olive grove, feeding her goats, when Alexis's House began to shake. The walls cracked, the chimney came down and the windows shattered, but, being well built and strong, it did not fall like so many houses on the island. Tiles fell, but the roof stayed on.

'Within an hour, Elena was there in Vathy town, helping to rescue people from their houses, reuniting bewildered children with their families, comforting those who were grieving over their dead. And she had her own family grieving to do. She soon learned the news that up in his village of Stavros, Manos's house was in ruins. He had escaped with Jason, your papa. But his wife Zita, your grandmother, had been killed.

'Elena brought the rest of the family back down from the ruins of Stavros to live with her in Alexis's House in the Valley of the Bells, where she looked after them. They were the first she took in, but they weren't the only ones. Word soon got about that Alexis's House had survived the earthquake, that there was shelter there and food, that with Elena they would be cared for.

'While the aftershocks lasted, many lived outside in the olive groves, not daring to go inside in case the house collapsed in the next aftershock. There was water in the well, enough olives and goat's cheese and honey to share out. There were more and more who needed help, and Elena welcomed as many in as she could. She especially loved hearing the sound of children's voices in Alexis's House, to watch them playing, knowing how much Alexis would have loved to have seen them there.

'Manos helped out all he could, as much as his bad leg would allow. But very soon, within days, he had made up his mind, as so many had, that with the

island in ruins, after invasion and occupation and now
earthquake, with grieving all about them, there was no
future on Ithaca. There were others going to Australia,
to a new land of hope and opportunity, a new life,
and he and Jason would be going with them.

'Elena did all she could to dissuade
him. She told him the two of them,
Manos and little Jason, could make
their home with her in Alexis's House.
Again and again, she tried to convince
him that he had to have faith, faith in
the spirit of Ithaca, that the island would
be rebuilt, that the island was the spirit of
its people, not its houses. But Manos would not
listen. Ithaca could never be rebuilt, he said. There'd
be no work, no life for Jason. They were going.

'He even tried to persuade Elena to come away with
them to Australia and make a new life for herself out
there, away from this island of suffering and sadness.

But she told him that Alexis was there with her in the house, that she would never leave him, never abandon Ithaca. It was her home, their home. She had fought for it; Manos had fought for it. Alexis and many others had died for it. No earthquake was going to drive her away. Besides, the islanders she had taken in needed her, needed Alexis's House until their own houses could be rebuilt.

'Brother and sister, much as they loved one another, soon knew they had come to a parting of the ways. The parting on the quayside in Vathy happened all too quickly. It was hard to bear for both of them. They knew it was unlikely they would ever see one another again. Australia was the other side of the world. Manos took the first boat that left Ithaca and emigrated with Jason – your papa. And, with hundreds of others from the islands, they sailed for their new life in Australia.'

I had to know. I had to ask, even though I knew how it might annoy him to be interrupted. 'So what happened to my grandpa, to Manos?' I said. 'They never told me.'

Proteus did not seem to be in the least annoyed.

'He died too young. It was the very day your papa left school. Some wounds, they never completely heal. His never did. Jason was alone now, but the community became his family. Your papa did well, worked hard, married your ma, and then you came along. You made your ma and papa very happy. You must always remember that. They lived for you. They still do.'

He fell silent, seeming to lose the thread of the story.

'Now, where was I?' he went on. 'Oh yes – after the parting on the quay, after Manos and little Jason left. Don't worry. It's a good story from now on. The best is yet to come. In the weeks that followed the terrible earthquake, your Auntie Ellie went on working wonders. Relief ships arrived to help the islanders, with food and water and medical supplies, with tents and blankets, but Alexis's House turned out to be one of the very few houses safe enough to live in. It became a refuge for the homeless and the hungry from all over the island. There were many islanders, many orphaned children amongst them, who lived for months and months afterwards under Elena's roof, or in tents in the olive grove. No one was ever turned away. Ithaca has never forgotten her kindnesses towards them.

'Elena had been right about the spirit of Ithaca and its people. The rubble and the ruins were cleared, houses everywhere were rebuilt, and the island came alive again. She stayed on in that big house, alone now, for years afterwards, long after everyone had gone. She missed the orphan children especially. They were the last to go, the last to be found homes.

'She was alone, but she never felt alone, for in that house Alexis was always with her. She never wanted to leave. But the house became too big for her to manage on her own, and it was too cold in the winter. She talked to Alexis, as she often did, and he agreed. It was time, time to go. She was too old to stay. Wherever she went, he told her, he would be with her. So she shut up the house and moved into Vathy, to the little house with the blue shutters on the harbour where she was born, where she grew up.

'Your Auntie Ellie, Nandi, she was a fighter for freedom, an angel of mercy, a hero as strong as Odysseus and as brave as Penelope. And there is more, much more, but not today. Later, later, tomorrow. I must go. I must go. I'm off. Fly me, Nandi, fly me.'

I released him the same way I released that stunned robin back home in Australia. I lifted him, then launched him up into the air to catch the wind, to give him flight, and away he went.

I know he'll be back tomorrow, and so will I. I must be. There's so much I want to ask him – one thing in particular, a favour – but each time I keep forgetting until he's gone, and then it's too late.

10 May

Pisaetos. By the port

This morning I walked out of town and along the coast road past Dexa Beach to the little white chapel where I think Elena and Alexis must have been married. It stood deep in an olive grove, with massive, ancient stones all around, just as Proteus had told me. I'm sure it was the place. I found it easily enough. Dozens of goats were picking their way down the track from the high hillside beyond the chapel, clambering in amongst the walls of ruins half buried by time. And then the whole herd was trotting across the road and up into the olive trees on the other side of the road.

They kept coming and they kept coming, the sound of their bells filling the hillside around me. There must have been a couple of hundred of them at least. They hardly noticed I was there, or they were ignoring me deliberately. As Proteus had once told me, goats seem to think they own the whole island. They have a right to think that. After all, they and their kind have been here since Odysseus and Penelope, and long before. They are as old as the hills, as old as the gods. I'm the newcomer here.

I wondered if the goats were passing by like this on the day Elena and Alexis were married. Who needs church bells when there are bells like these? And were they bleating their congratulations as the couple came out of that little chapel door, hand in hand, into the sunlight?

The chapel was simple inside and tiny, barely room for a dozen people. I lit a candle for them and sat there, trying and failing to picture how it must have been, how happy and hopeful they must have felt that day, how Elena might have looked then, all those years before she became my ancient Auntie Ellie. I was suddenly overwhelmed with sadness at the thought of the life together they had not had the chance to live, and I had to leave.

I walked on down the hill after that to the port at Pisaetos, looking all along the verges for those flowers Alexis had picked and given to Elena after their wedding. What were they called? Wild gladioli – no, purple gladioli, that's it. I didn't find any, which was disappointing.

That's where I am now, at the port of Pisaetos, sitting writing my diary on the quayside where the boats come in from Kefallonia. I came here because I needed to look out to sea across the strait to Kefallonia. On the map

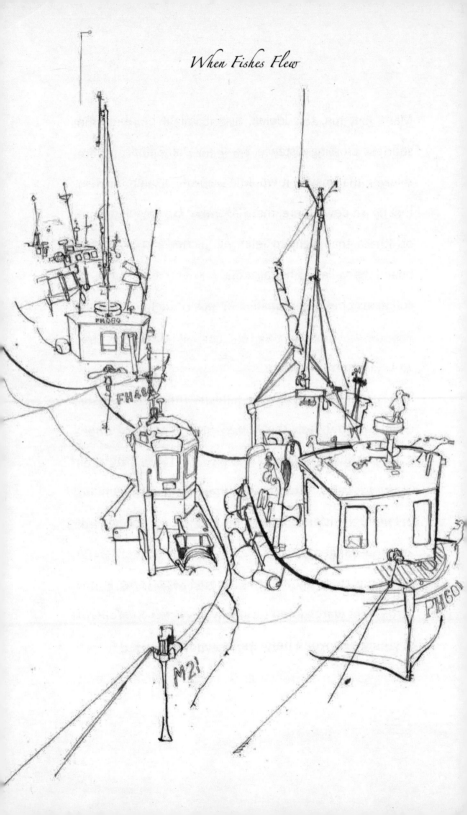

Maria lent me, this looked as if it might be about the shortest crossing-distance between the islands. So I'm thinking that maybe it would have been around here, on that beach down there, that Elena must have swum ashore on Ithaca that night to fetch her father and his fishing boat. I marvelled at her again, at her feat of strength and courage, at her determination to make it across, to rescue Alexis and Manos from the shores of Kefallonia.

Even from here on the quayside, you can see how strong the currents are out in the middle of the channel, how fast the waters are running through it, how rough the waves are, even today with the sea quite calm. What is it – three, maybe four miles between the islands here? I can only imagine how hard and how dangerous such a swim must have been. Elena really did that, my amazing Auntie Ellie. Looking out across that water, I don't think I've ever felt so proud of anything or anyone before in my whole life.

Afternoon of the same day. Alexis's House

On the way back to Dexa Beach from Pisaetos, I got a lift in a minibus carrying tourists, some of them English, some American. I didn't hitch. The minibus just stopped, and the driver told me to hop in. I didn't remember his name, but I knew him from the party in the restaurant, and he knew me, greeting me like an old friend.

I discovered the tourists had all come to Ithaca to look for wild flowers. One of them, the one I was sitting next to, a formidable old lady from Yorkshire in England, told me they had just been walking up in the hills near Homer's house. Yesterday they had been to Kefallonia, on those same hills where Elena and Manos and Alexis had fought so hard for freedom, and where

Alexis and so many of their partisan friends had died. And I was thinking: here we were, all of us in this bus, enjoying that freedom, and just how lucky we were. I told the old lady from England, because she asked, that I was on Ithaca researching my family history.

She said she could tell from my accent that I must be from New Zealand. I told her I was from Australia, from Melbourne, but she didn't hear me. I think she loved to talk rather than listen. She had been to New Zealand, she went on, studying wild flowers. Lovely country, she told me, glorious flowers. I told her again I was Australian, but Greek too, that Australia has lovely flowers too.

'Well, you don't sound Australian or Greek,' she said. 'Lovely country, Greece,' she went on. 'But I don't like the cheese. And they eat too much squid. Calamari. Calamari, every meal. And that retsina wine! Tastes like paint stripper. How do they drink the stuff!'

I asked her then if she'd ever found any wild purple

gladioli on the island. She put her hand on my arm. 'So you love them too! That's wonderful.' She seemed almost tearful. 'They're everywhere in the hills. You can find them easily up above Dexa Beach. A bit of a climb, but it's worth it. Came across a whole field of them up there, a field of purple. Magnificent. I think they must be the flower most loved by the gods, don't you? My favourite flower in all the world. And you love them too. Kindred spirits then. Well, I never. I have a kindred spirit from New Zealand.'

I said nothing. There wasn't any point.

I asked the driver to drop me off at Dexa Beach. The sun was still high, and hot too – too hot! I had time enough to look for that field of purple gladioli the talkative tourist lady had told me about. As she had said, it was a steep climb, but it was worth it. The flowers seemed to glow in the sunlight. I never saw such intense colour, such brightness. I thought then how wonderful it would be one day to teach myself to paint them. I had to drag myself away. I had to see

Alexis's House, to see the place for myself, to go inside maybe, explore it.

I'd only had that distant glimpse of it through the trees from the hillside above. I still had time. I had to have a closer look.

So that's why I'm here now, sitting writing this, in a rickety old chair I found in the kitchen – it was easy to get in. The house is hidden deep in the Valley of the Bells, entirely surrounded by trees and undergrowth. Even from inside the house I can hear goats and their bells all around. It looks as if no one has been in here for years. I wouldn't have gone in, but one of the doors was off its hinges, and no one was about. It's so strange being here, knowing so much about the life of the place, about Alexis and Auntie Ellie, all the people who have lived here, been sheltered here.

Just a few weeks, that was all the short life they were granted in this place, Alexis and Elena. Why did the gods do that to them? Proteus will know. I'll ask him.

And all those people, those children that Auntie Ellie had taken in and cared for after the earthquake, where were they now? Had any of them been at my surprise welcoming party? Some were certainly old enough. No wonder everyone there seemed to love her so much. Sitting here, I understand so well why Maria and Costas, and so many others, treat me as kindly as they do. I live in the glow of their love for Elena, for my Auntie Ellie. They all seem to think she'll be home soon. I hope they're right. I so hope they're right.

11 May

Dawn over Vathy. About my yesterday

I've hardly slept thinking about yesterday. The chapel, the port at Pisaetos, Alexis's House. And then there was my meeting with Proteus that evening.

I'm finding it difficult to know what to call people in my diary. I keep chopping and changing. I've decided Auntie Ellie should stay Auntie Ellie. I can't get used to Elena. It's their name for her. They love her as Elena. I love her as Auntie Ellie. And my flying fish will be Proteus because he speaks to me as a god, the god who has brought me here. The flying fish is his form, not his being. So he's always Proteus from now on.

I didn't get down to the jetty in time yesterday. I fell

asleep in Alexis's House. I think it was all that walking and those bells outside lulling me to sleep. Anyway, when I woke, the sun was already below the hill, and the warmth of the day was fading. I had to run all the way there, across the road, through the olive grove. The family at the far end of the beach wasn't there. No one was. I stood at the end of the jetty, the evening wind whipping up the sea. The wind always seems to get up towards the end of the day. I was suddenly cold.

Proteus wasn't there either. The little black fish were. They seemed to be waiting not so much for me but for my feet to nibble. So I sat down and dangled my feet and wiggled my toes. I don't know why I did it. The tune just came into my head, from the party, I suppose. 'Zorba's Dance'. The tune was so catchy and I loved it. I lifted my hands above my head and began clicking my fingers just as Auntie Ellie used to do. I began to hum it softly, swaying to it, my feet moving to the rhythm

of it under the water, stirring up those inquisitive little black fish.

I heard his whispering voice before I saw him. 'Mikis Theodorakis!'

It was Proteus, leaping up from the water nearby,

and high into the air above me. I held out my hands instinctively, caught him and held him as he fell into them.

'Like Elena, I love that man, I love his music,' he said and, settling his wet wings in amongst my fingers, he began to hum along with me. He hummed huskily but tunefully. We sounded quite good together, a great duet. And we laughed together when we finished.

'I'm sorry I'm late, Nandi,' he began, 'but I've had a busy day. A long flight, a long swim out to the open sea, but I found what I was looking for, saw who I was looking for. So it was worth it. And you've been busy too, haven't you?'

And he proceeded to tell me everywhere I had been, everything I'd done, reminding me that he was an omnipresent god, as well as a flying fish. 'And now here you are, humming Mikis Theodorakis. Elena would have loved that so much. I must tell you about Elena and Theodorakis. She knew him, you know. They met once, after they both came out of prison. He was, he is, a great hero of hers. You know all about heroes, don't you, Nandi? Well, this man, Mikis Theodorakis, is Elena's modern-day hero.'

'Auntie Ellie was in prison?' I interrupted, and immediately regretted it.

'If you listen, I'll tell you all about it. Are you listening or interrupting?'

I nodded, shamefaced, but willing him to go on.

'You may not know this. I do. All gods do. People quickly forget their history, and their stories, which means, of course, they forget themselves, and then very often they go on to make the same mistakes all over again. We gods, we see it all the time. Like all countries, Greece has had her glory times: her philosophers, her architects, her poetry and plays; and then her sad times: invasion, occupation, earthquake, disease and tyranny. In the good times, the happy times, in times of freedom, people forget these things. Gods never forget.

'It was a while after the earthquake, in 1967, that a new sadness came to Greece, a new tyranny. It spread to every corner of Greece, every island, to Ithaca. The tyrants were home-made this time, not invaders. They called themselves the Colonels. These were not foreign tyrants, but Greek tyrants. Like all such men, they wanted to control people's lives and thoughts. They banned everything and everyone they did not like, who disagreed with them. They banned democracy, banished free speech from Greece.

'Ithaca was rebuilding itself from the rubble. Houses and churches and schools and a health centre were growing up out of the ruins. But it was all taking a long time, and was hard for the people. There was still hunger and poverty on the island. Many, as you know, had already left because it had become a sad place to be, an island with no prospects: little food, little money, little hope. Many islanders had followed Manos and Jason to Australia.

'But, all this while, Elena had stayed on in Alexis's House, looking after those children who still needed a roof over their heads, looking after her olive trees, and her bees and her hens, and her sheep and goats too.

'Like many on the island, Elena put up with the

Colonels reluctantly, angrily, trying to get on with her life, ignoring as best she could their idiotic, tyrannical rules. She had her 'family', as she called them, to look after. All over the island people did much the same, and hoped things would get better. But they didn't. Everything became worse, a lot worse. The Colonels began to ban certain books and plays, great Greek writers, Socrates and Sophocles amongst them. They dictated how people should dress, and they banned the letter Z. Honestly, they did! And then they decided to ban the singing of the music of Mikis Theodorakis, and they put him in prison. They put lots of people in prison they didn't like. They were good at that.

'For Elena, when she heard the news of this, that was a step too far. She decided enough was enough, that something had to be done. So she went and stood outside the police station in Vathy, and she sang all the Theodorakis songs she knew, and that was all of them, not just 'Zorba's Dance'.

'A crowd gathered. Soon half the town was there, and singing and dancing with her. But not everyone was singing and dancing. These Colonels had their supporters everywhere, even in Ithaca.The police arrested Elena, took her away, put her on a boat to the mainland. She was in prison there for three months, in the same prison for a while as Mikis Theodorakis. They met there, and that was one of the great moments of her life.

'When the Colonels' regime fell, as all tyrants must fall, and democracy and freedom were finally restored, Elena came home to Ithaca, to a hero's welcome from the islanders. There never was a homecoming like it. They sang the songs of freedom, danced and drank and broke many plates, as Greeks do when they celebrate. They have lost it enough, so they know that nothing is better to celebrate than freedom.'

Proteus could hardly lift his voice to a whisper by now. 'I must go,' he said. 'Even the gods tire. And I will not come again, Nandi. I do not need to. My work here is done. You know what you must know. You will do with it what you will. But do not imagine the story is over. It is your story. From now on, you do the telling. Make the best of it, Nandi, and look after her.'

I did not have to be asked. I knew it was the moment. I opened my hands and he left me. He flew away like a bird, then dived and became a fish and vanished into the sea. But he is not a bird, or a fish, or a flying fish. He is Proteus, son of Poseidon, and a god. And we have been friends.

Once he had gone, I remembered again the many questions I had been longing to ask him. Why do the gods let terrible things happen in the world? Why is there so much sadness? Why did Alexis have to be killed? Why could he and Auntie Ellie not have had a life of peace and happiness together? And then there was the most important question of all I needed to ask him, but it was too late now even to ask that. Or I thought it was.

His whispering words came back to me in reply over the waves, from far away , like a murmur, like a song of the sea. 'There are no answers, Nandi, only questions. We gods live alongside you, in amongst you. We do not interfere. Well, not often – only when we feel like it.'

I cupped my hands to my mouth and shouted my question out over the sea as loudly as I could.

'Proteus! Proteus! If you can hear me, let me ask you one question. I have no one else who can help me. Will you bring Auntie Ellie home safe and soon? You know how much I want to see her. Please help her come home. I want you to interfere. You did when you swam alongside her that night across the channel. You felt like it then. I'm asking you, Proteus, to feel like helping her again. Please, as a favour to me?'

I waited, and I waited, but in reply there was only the sound of the waves rolling gently in over the pebbles.

12 May

A different bedroom. In Auntie Ellie's house. Night-time

It all began early. Maria knocked on my door and told me I had to come quickly. I thought something must be wrong. I could hear in her voice that she was holding back tears. Outside, as we hurried along, it was barely light. The town was dawn-still and asleep all around us. But out in the harbour I could see the lights of a boat coming in, a large boat, one of the ferries maybe.

Maria was holding my hand, tight, not just to hurry me on but for comfort. I could feel it. I tried to ask what was wrong, but she could only shake her head, look away and cry into her handkerchief. The boat had docked by the time we got there, and people were getting off.

Then I saw her. Auntie Ellie! Auntie Ellie was coming down the gangplank, stepping carefully. And she was not alone. She was carrying one small child and leading another by the hand.

Maria was grasping my arm. '*Dóxa to Theó*,' she was whispering through her tears. '*Dóxa to Theó*.' I knew what that meant by now. Thank God. So I thanked God too, all of the gods, but Proteus in particular, in Greek and in English.

Auntie Ellie saw me and recognised me at once, almost as if she was looking out for me. She called to me with such joy in her voice. 'Nandi! Nandi!'

I waved back. I couldn't speak.

Then she was standing there in front of me, old but no older, but smaller than I remembered, and introducing me to the two little girls. 'Maya, this is your new sister, Nandi. And, Hala, say hello to Nandi, your new sister.

Maya and Hala are from Syria. And, children, Nandi is your big sister from Australia.'

And then Auntie Ellie put Hala down, took my face in her hands and kissed me on both cheeks and on the forehead. 'I knew you would come one day,' she said.

'And I knew it would be today. Don't ask me how, but I knew.'

'So did I,' I replied, only just managing to speak. 'I think I have really come home,' I told her.

'And Hala and Maya have come home too,' my Auntie Ellie said, 'home to Ithaca. All of you home to Ithaca, and to Alexis and me.'

As we were walking back along the harbour wall in the first light of a new dawn towards Maria's house, Auntie Ellie reached out and held my hand, swinging it just as she used to in Melbourne when I was little, beside the Yarra River.

There was no one else about – it was that early. I thought we were alone. But I was wrong. Out of the still waters of the harbour there leaped a flying fish, once, twice, and again and again, until we had all seen it, and marvelled at it, Auntie Ellie, Maria, Maya and Hala too.

Me too. Me most of all. He was a god of his word.

Not the end, a new beginning

Ten years on

I have long wanted to write this story. It's taken me a while. You may think it all rather fantastical. Well, you think what you like. But I'm telling you it was the flying fish that brought me to Ithaca. Then, as I later learned – and I didn't doubt it anyway – everything Proteus told me about Auntie Ellie turned out to be true. All the exploits and stories of her extraordinary life were confirmed by Maria and by many others on the island later. The life of Auntie Ellie is no myth.

To reread my diary of those few days long ago, when I was seventeen, is to know that coming here to find

Auntie Ellie changed the course of my whole life. I have not a doubt in my mind that it was destined, meant, fate – call it what you will – that one way or the other it was arranged by the gods – actually by one god, who was a flying fish.

I have stayed on in Ithaca, living with Auntie Ellie, being a big sister to her two adopted Syrian refugee children, Maya and Hala. They were orphans rescued from the sea. They were found clinging to a rubber boat off the Greek island of Lesvos, where so many refugees arrive from the coast of Turkey, all of them desperate for a home, for safety from war and hunger. They had nothing: no home, no family, no country. Only their names. Now they have a home and a family. Their family is my family. Their home is the island of Ithaca.

I found out later that Auntie Ellie, old as she was, had gone off from time to time to look after children in a refugee camp on the island of Lesvos. She believes deeply that nothing in the world matters more than the lives of children, and that it was the right of every child to have a family, to belong, that to live unwanted in this world, especially when they had seen what they had seen, was wrong, simply wrong. She found Maya and Hala, who had no one in this world. They were to her the children Alexis and she would have had. She didn't need to tell me that. I knew.

They had come, Auntie Ellie told me, from the bombed-out town of Azaz in the north of Syria. Their father was killed there, buried under the rubble of their house. The rest of the family had made their way through village after village in the countryside around Idlib, and finally crossed over the border into Turkey, then gone by bus to the coast. They lost their mother when their rubber boat overturned in heavy seas on the way to Lesvos.

How long they had been clinging to the boat no one knew. They were near death when they were found. They had been in a refugee camp after that for more than a year. No one wanted them. But Auntie Ellie wanted them, wanted to bring them home to Ithaca to live with her. Only the authorities kept saying she was too old to care for them. And she kept insisting that you're never too old to care, and in the end they had no answer to that.

With the help of friends from all over the island, we restored Alexis's House and moved in. It took a while – there was a lot to do. It's been home to Auntie Ellie and me and the children ever since. We harvest the olives, keep a few sheep and goats, and hens – Maya and Hala love the hens.

Every year on Auntie Ellie's wedding anniversary, we all get in a flotilla of little boats, family and friends, and go across the channel to Kefallonia, each of us taking a bunch of purple gladioli. All the way over there, I think of Ellie swimming across on that moonlit night during the German occupation all those long years ago, and I marvel at it, at her.

We get in taxis then, and go to the church where

Alexis is buried. We lay our gladioli on his grave so that it is purple-high with flowers, and leave Auntie Ellie alone with him for a few minutes. In the evening, we have a party in Alexis's House, and the music plays, and we sing and we dance, always with many echoes of *Zorba the Greek* and Mikis Theodorakis.

Auntie Ellie remains strong to this day, I think because she is happy, happy to be back where she was with Alexis, happy to be loved by her children and her family, by the whole community. She still gets her dizzy spells and, because her eyesight is weak, she prefers to be read to than to read herself. I do that. She did it for me once. I think it is her voice telling me stories and meaning every word, living every word, that made me want to be a writer. She's often coming out with vivid memories she likes to tell me about. I think she's passing them on to me, making them my memories too. I love that.

She still swims on Dexa Beach summer and winter, every afternoon. And I go with her. Hala and Maya and I clean the beach every day, Auntie Ellie sometimes too, though she finds bending more difficult these days. There's not once that I go down to the beach with her and the children to swim that I don't look out for a flying fish. I've never seen one again.

When we celebrated her ninety-eighth birthday,

only yesterday, she was wearing the blue-and-yellow scarf I knitted for her in Australia and brought with me in my rucksack to give her. We played her Theodorakis music and she watched us dance, her two little Greek-Syrian girls loving every moment of it, as I did. And when she got up and swayed to the music, swathed in her blue-and-yellow scarf, a great cheer went up that must have echoed all the way to Australia.

After the party, I was walking her slowly, arm in arm, into the house. She had not spoken for some time and seemed tired. She stopped and turned to me. I knew a story was coming.

'Nandi,' she said. 'There's something I don't think I've ever told you. It's on my mind now and I must. It was when I was at sea on my way home, bringing the girls back with me – years ago now, you remember? It happened just the evening before we met you on the quayside. A terrible storm came up. The skies blackened above the ship; the wind roared. It was the worst storm

I had ever known, waves as high as a house. We were being tossed about like a cork. I thought the boat must go down. Everyone did. I held the two girls tight and prayed. Never had I prayed so hard in all my life, Nandi. And then suddenly it was over, as suddenly as it had begun. It was as if the gods were watching over us. I'm so glad they were, else I'd never have seen you again. And you are very dear to me, Nandi. I think the gods knew that. I wanted you to know.'

I had always wondered over all these years if Proteus really had helped bring her safely home to me, to Ithaca. Now I knew for sure.

As for me now, when I'm not painting walls, or mending the drains, or fixing the plumbing, I look after Maya and Hala, taking them to school, playing with them, reading to them, feeding them, and I look after the olive trees, and the hens, and the bees, and the vegetables and the goats. And on summer evenings, with the breeze coming in off the sea, I sit outside with Auntie Ellie in our Valley of the Bells, and listen to the sheep and goats grazing on the hillside, and I remember. I remember her story, and my story. Our story now.

And, when I go up to my bedroom, there's my glowing globe and my Odysseus statue and my silver dolphin. I still treasure them. But I have another hero these days, who couldn't be less like Odysseus. Should I call her hero or heroine? She wouldn't want me to call her either.

I do a lot of painting these days – those purple gladioli started that – and, as you have realised, I write books too, stories for children and for grown-up children, and sometimes I do the illustrations too. So, between my painting and my writing, I can earn just about enough to invite Ma and Papa over here from Australia to stay for two or three months every year in the summer. They come to live with us here, in Alexis's House – there's plenty of room. They know Auntie

Ellie's life story now, but we never speak of any of it in front of her. She knows we know, and we know she knows we know, and we all know she's happier if we never speak of it. So we don't.

Ma and Papa are here with us on the island right now. Most days we all go down to Dexa Beach together to swim, Auntie Ellie in her black dress and black headscarf. And every now and then she still wanders up and down the shore, picking up any washed-up plastic. On chillier days, she'll sit on the beach in my yellow-and-blue scarf, watching Maya and Hala leaping off the jetty, screeching and screaming, full of the joys of life. They love to dive down, looking for the little black fish.

Today I stayed on after they'd all left and gone back to the house. I like my quiet times. I went, as I sometimes do, and sat there alone at the end of the jetty, swinging my feet in the water for a while, remembering. I looked for him. I always do. He didn't come. He never does.

My Odyssey

The little black fish were there though, nibbling at my toes. But they don't bite. I was never happier.

I have the best of all worlds.

Dóxa to Theó.

The End

ITALY

SICILY

Ithaca

GRE

MEDITERRANEAN